PENGUIN BOOKS

THE BLOOD PRINCE OF LANGKASUKA

Tutu Dutta lives in Kuala Lumpur; she was born in India but grew up in Malaysia. She has a BSc from Universiti Putra Malaysia and an MPhil from the University of Malaya. As an undergraduate, she won a scholarship from Japan Airlines, to attend Summer School at Sophia University in Tokyo, an eye-opening experience which instilled in her a love for folklore. She has also studied at the University of Strasbourg, France.

Dutta started writing children's books when she lived in far flung cities as the spouse of a diplomat, including: Singapore, Lagos, New York, Havana and Zagreb. She has a daughter, Shona Yean, who was born in Singapore in 1992. Shona is her informant on youth and popular culture and keeps her abreast of international trends; Shona qualified as a Barrister at Middle Temple Inn (UK) in 2017.

To date, Tutu Dutta has authored nine books, including *Timeless Tales of Malaysia*, *Eight Treasures of the Dragon*, and the middle grade duology, *The Jugra Chronicles*, a story set in 17th Century Borneo. *Phoenix Song* is her first picture book; published by Lantana Publishing (UK) and illustrated by Martina Peluso. It is also her first book, to be translated into Malay, and was published by Oyez! in 2017.

In 2016, Marshall Cavendish decided to publish a new edition of *Timeless Tales of Malaysia*, entitled *The Magic Urn and Other Timeless Tales of Malaysia*. This was followed by *Nights of the Dark Moon*, a collection of dark folktales from Asia and Africa, in 2017. It was reprinted in 2019 and garnered renewed interest and positive media reviews in Malaysia and India.

In 2019, an anthology she co-edited with Sharifah Aishah Osman, entitled *The Principal Girl: Feminist Tales from Asia*, was published by GB Gerakbudaya Enterprise Sdn Bhd, a publisher known for social activism. This book was a surprise hit with YA readers and received wide media coverage and reviews.

She was invited as a speaker at the Asian Festival of Children's Content in Singapore, twice. The first in 2013, where she presented a paper entitled Adapting Asian Folktales for Children's and YA

Literature, and in 2017 she presented two papers, Folklore Finesse and Hidden Elements. She was also one of the speakers at a panel of Malaysian authors during the East-West Conference organized by the University of Malaya in 2017.

Tutu Dutta was also one of the judges for the Scholastic Asia Young Writers Award 2014, representing Malaysia. Her stories are rooted in Asian culture and reflect the research she had put into the subject. Readers and reviewers have also pointed out the feminist leanings and the deep reverence for nature, in her stories. In fact, *Timeless Tales of Malaysia*, inspired a group of children to produce a video about it and was the subject of a Master's Degree in English Literature at the University of Malaya.

She is active in local literary circles and is a Committee Member of the Malaysian Writers Society, helmed by Tina Isaac and Gina Yap, since its inception in 2017; and also a member and Patron of The Classic Challengers, a readers and writers collective, helmed by Nazli Anim Ghazali and Vickneswaran Manickasagar.

The Blood Prince of Langkasuka

TUTU DUTTA

PENGUIN BOOKS

An imprint of Penguin Random House

PENGUIN BOOKS

USA | Canada | UK | Ireland | Australia
New Zealand | India | South Africa | China | Southeast Asia

Penguin Books is part of the Penguin Random House group of companies whose addresses can be found at global.penguinrandomhouse.com

Published by Penguin Random House SEA Pte Ltd
9, Changi South Street 3, Level 08-01,
Singapore 486361

First published in Penguin Books by Penguin Random House SEA 2020

Copyright © Tutu Dutta 2020

All rights reserved

10 9 8 7 6 5 4 3 2 1

This is a work of fiction. Names, characters, places and incidents are either the product of the author's imagination or are used fictitiously and any resemblance to any actual person, living or dead, events or locales is entirely coincidental.

ISBN 9789814882927

Typeset in Adobe Caslon Pro by Manipal Technologies Limited, Manipal

This book is sold subject to the condition that it shall not, by way of trade or otherwise, be lent, resold, hired out, or otherwise circulated without the publisher's prior consent in any form of binding or cover other than that in which it is published and without a similar condition including this condition being imposed on the subsequent purchaser.

www.penguin.sg

This book is dedicated to my husband, Dato' Yean Yoke Heng, and to my daughter, Shona Yean, Barrister-at-Law; both who have supported me in one way or the other and made my life as a writer possible.

And to my parents, Dr Kanak Shankar Dutta, a lifelong reader, and my mother, Mrs Chingkang Hangsheng Dutta, who disdained reading.

And also to all the children of the Yean, Dutta and Hangsheng clans . . .

Contents

The Night of the Blood Moon	1
The Ruined Temple	11
The Cook's Tale	23
The Hunt	33
The Bamboo Princess	49
The Handmaiden's Tale	70
Maharaja Lela Seeks the Truth	88
The Moon Garden	103
The Story of the Temple Maiden	121
An Ancient Curse	139
The Traitor	146
The Village on the Hill	161
Acknowledgements	171

The Night of the Blood Moon

He sighed with exasperation, narrowing his eyes until only dark irises were visible and a slight frown creased the perfection of his smooth brow. Raja Maha Perita Deria, prince of the blood and heir to the throne of Langkasuka, was getting irritated. When he spoke, his smooth and cultured voice was devastatingly contemptuous, 'Why are we taking so long? We are merely dressing for a night in the town, not for battle!'

His servant, a nervous young man, was helping him to put on his bracelets. Ornate curling fern leaves were to circle each arm, wrought in gold and studded with tiny diamonds to mimic spores. They tended to draw attention but the prince was reckless in his indifference to danger. Situated on a hill overlooking the sea to the West, the town of Kota Aur had its fair share of brigands and robbers, and even some pirates, but Raja Perita was confident that no one would dare to challenge him and even if they did, he could outfight most of them.

The servant finally managed to close the catch of the bracelet on his right arm but his fingers fumbled with the catch on the second bracelet. Sensing Raja Perita's growing impatience, his hands trembled even more and beads of sweat formed on his brow. When he tried to close the catch, the bracelet dropped on the floor with a heavy thud. The prince said brusquely, 'Must you be so clumsy? Why do I always have to put up with such incompetence?'

The servant, who was kneeling on the floor to pick up the jewel, apologized, his voice quavering, 'Please forgive me, my lord! Your humble slave promises to do better . . .'

Raja Perita held up his hand and said imperiously, 'Enough! Just put it away and leave us! I can dress myself!'

In fact, he was already dressed in sleeveless tunic and loose black silk trousers. On top of the trousers, a brocaded green silk scarf was elegantly draped around his waist and held in place by a silver belt. The two ends of the cloth fell in front in carefully folded pleats. The prince threw on his outer garment, a jacket of matching green silk and strode out of the palace determinedly. The magnificent wooden palace rested at the very top of Kota Aur, and was nestled in the midst of a lush garden of rare flowering plants, orchids and ferns, and tall shady flowering trees. A stream, bearing crystal clear water, flowed downhill at one end of the garden into a rock pool. A high wooden parapet surrounded the sprawling palace grounds.

The cool evening air refreshed him and Raja Perita walked down the tree-lined path in the garden in a much better mood. The garden path led to the rear gate of the palace. Outside the gate, another path led down the hill to the town. Closest to the palace, resided the *bangsawan*, the lesser royalty and nobility of Langkasuka. A second, larger circle comprised dwellings owned by wealthy merchants and palace retainers.

Towards the west where the port was, were warehouses, a metal smithing foundry and a few brick-firing kilns. Tall shady trees grew everywhere, even around the foundry and kilns and gave Kota Aur the look of a massive landscaped garden. On the eastern side of the hill were tradesmen and their shops, elegant teahouses and spacious temples with courtyards.

Further inland were the villages and extensive rice fields, laid out with checkerboard precision. Furthest of all were the dark primal forests, with green tendrils snaking their way into human settlements. The town was called Kota Aur or Bamboo City because the site used to be covered with bamboo forests; *aur* being the name of a giant species of bamboo which grew to massive heights with stems the size of a man's thigh. The giant bamboo forest had been felled a long time ago but vestiges of it still remained in the untouched forest which surrounded the kingdom.

Although it was after nightfall, a full blood moon illuminated the terrain with startling clarity. Three young men were waiting for Raja Perita at the palace gates, their elegant dress and casually confident bearing signalled them out as noblemen of the kingdom of Langkasuka. Chula, Satra and Yala were young noblemen who had a penchant for night life; they were also his closest friends. The prince told the guards to wait for him at the gate—he didn't want them to follow him. The four friends divided their time between hunting in the forest and frequenting teahouses owned by rich merchants from across the sea. The prince and his friends were popular in the teahouses and always welcomed.

They were young and carefree; with dark shiny eyes, tawny skin and lean strong limbs from hours spent outdoors. All four were admired for their physical prowess; they were proficient with weapons and accomplished hunters. But none was as skilled as Raja Perita; his prowess bordered on the preternatural. Many say it was a legacy from his mother, who was rumoured to be a *rakshasa* princess. Others say she was descended from the *orang Bunyan*, the fair folk. The more prosaic even claimed that she was an *orang Hulu* princess, a member of the hill tribe from Mount Jerai; but whatever her origins, no one disputed her extraordinary beauty. His father, Raja Seri Indrawangsa, was descended from the most ancient ruling house in the land. While both parents were proud of their only son, they often wished that Raja Perita would mend his wild and reckless ways.

The prince turned towards his companions and asked rhetorically, 'Who shall we honour with our presence tonight?' His voice had a rich timbre which contrasted with his youthful looks; in fact, he was only seventeen years old and the second youngest in the group.

Chula replied, 'The moon tonight is blood red in colour, my lord. I would advise caution. We should stick to our favourite haunt, the Green Jade teahouse close by.'

Yala burst out laughing, his eyes alight with amusement. He was the wild child of the group, outgoing and free spirited. He said boisterously, 'Chula is always advising caution, even when there is no moon at all! I say we go to the Whispering Bamboo teahouse at the edge of town!'

'I've never heard of this teahouse before . . . is it new?' Satra asked, sounding intrigued. Yala always seemed to know what was going on in Kota Aur and always came up with the wild ideas. He could be impatient and disdainful, but he was never boring.

Yala said with good-humoured contempt, 'You're such a hermit, Satra! The Whispering Bamboo teahouse has been around for ages.' He lowered his voice and whispered, 'We should really pay it a visit . . . especially since rumour has it that the forest near the teahouse is haunted by a *puaka* which takes the form of a beautiful young woman . . .'

This time Chula interjected in a sharp voice, 'Yala! Why would you even suggest such a frightful idea on a night like this . . .'

Before he could finish the sentence, a sudden gust of wind blew around them, rustling the leaves in the nearby trees and shaking lose white scented flowers. The prince felt a stir in his heart and his pulse quickened. He suddenly decided to agree with Yala, 'Life has been so stifling lately, I could do with a bit of adventure. Let's go to the Whispering Bamboo teahouse!'

While Chula looked exasperated, the other three bantered cheerfully along the road between rows of imposing wooden houses, shuttered for the night. Yala guided them down one narrow alley after another until they arrived close to the teahouse at the edge of the town. The houses here were smaller and the teahouse was the only one which was brightly lit with lamps. Led by the prince, they sauntered into the Whispering Bamboo teahouse with their heads held high. Raja Perita always managed to give the impression that he owned the place. However, they were surprised to find that they were the only customers. A tall man with a pale complexion, dressed in a black silk robe characteristic of the wealthy Tang traders, appeared from behind a screen and welcomed them with an obsequious bow, 'Welcome to my humble teahouse, young lords! Allow me to show you to my best tea room!' His voice had the sing song lilt all Tang people seemed to have.

He led them to a private room which had a low wooden platform at one end. Low steps flanked by ornately carved banisters led up the platform, where the steps ended, the banisters encircled it. The rest of the room was empty, except for six large drums which were placed along the walls. Waving his hand with a flourish, he bowed to them again. Although they had never met before, the man had no difficulty identifying Raja Perita as the leader of the group. The man said in an ingratiating voice, 'I trust that you find this humble room acceptable, my lord! Please seat yourself. A serving woman will be here with refreshments soon.'

The platform was covered with a fine woven mat, and there was a low rectangular table in polished black lacquer placed in the middle. Four cushions in black silk embroidered with bamboo motifs in white silk had been placed on the floor around the table. Raja Perita was impressed—he didn't expect the place to be so well appointed. The four friends climbed up the stairs and sat on the cushions and waited to be served. When the owner was out of earshot, Yala remarked with a hint of sarcasm, 'A man with disconcertingly refined manners!'

Chula said with a smile, 'For once, I agree with you, Yala!'

A young woman dressed in a jade green silk robe arrived soon after and served them hot aromatic tea in delicate porcelain cups. She was slender, with large dark eyes, but her complexion was as wan as the teahouse owner and contrasted sharply with her bright robe. Raja Perita wondered how someone so young could be so lacklustre, but she was undeniably beautiful. They thanked her politely and she bowed gracefully and left the room.

Satra remarked, 'I never knew the maidens of Kota Aur could be so elegant; she puts some of the high-born palace ladies to shame!'

The prince commented offhandedly, 'She is beautiful, but rather insipid . . .'

Chula raised an eyebrow at his remark, then shrugged and said, 'Just like weak tea, I suppose . . . although I rather favour that type of look. Anyway, come dear friends; let us enjoy our hot tea before it becomes tepid!' They proceeded to sip their tea. He sighed contentedly and said, 'This is divine! There is something about tea which makes me feel content and at peace.'

Yala commented, 'You're such a maiden, Chula! Personally, I prefer something a little stronger . . . but the Queen has forbidden us from drinking when the prince is around.'

Raja Perita gave him a sidelong glance but chose to ignore his remark. The arrival of a steaming basket of dumplings filled with roasted duck meat caught their attention and made them forget about the banter. The dumplings were accompanied by another basket of steamed rice wrapped in lotus leaf filled with mushrooms and beans. It was delicious and the four friends ate with gusto. The last course was little cakes filled with ground lotus paste sweetened with brown sugar. Satra commented while helping himself to another piece of cake, 'This lotus cake is delicious! We were right to come here; the food is even better than the Green Jade!'

The prince said with a trace of sarcasm, 'It should be, considering they only have four customers to feed . . . not much going on in the way of entertainment though.'

As if in response to his comment, three young women dressed in bright silk robes glided into the room. Each was dressed in a different colour: red, pink and orange. They were followed by a young man dressed in black tunic and trousers. The young man took his position behind one of the drums and started beating the drum slowly—the sound was rhythmic and mellow. The dancers followed in step gracefully, waving their long elegant sleeves around into intricate patterns. As the pace of the drumbeats increased, the swirling sleeves and robes flew around like flower blossoms scattering in the wind. The four young men stopped eating to enjoy the show. Abruptly, the drumbeats stopped and the maidens stopped dancing. Instead they started to sing—their voices a high nasal falsetto. The prince and his friends looked alarmed; finally one of them burst out laughing. It was Yala. Raja Perita sat up abruptly and held up his hand. He said sharply, 'Stop! Stop singing now! I can't stand that awful screeching!'

The dancers stopped singing, looking confused and dismayed. One of them asked in a halting voice, 'Did we offend you, my lord?'

Before the prince could reply, Chula interjected, 'No, not at all, dear ladies! We just prefer to watch you dance, that's all!'

The dancers looked at one another, and then at the drummer. He nodded and the dancer in red walked towards the drum on the opposite side of the room. The two of them started to beat their drums but the rhythm was faster and much more energetic. The two remaining dancers threw away their robes. The four friends were surprised to see that they were wearing matching loose trousers and tunics below the robes. The two dancers jumped into the air and landed in an acrobatic handstand before flipping on their feet again. They did several somersaults and incredible flips through the air in time to the drum beats. The four friends watched open-mouthed until the acrobatic dance was over. The four friends, even the normally nonchalant prince, cheered and clapped in appreciation. They threw silver coins towards the dancers, who literally flew around and caught them adeptly without letting a single coin fall on the floor. Then the dancers and drummers bowed out of the room.

New dishes were served and a different serving maid, not as pale nor as pretty as the first one, stayed on to pour them their tea. The four friends settled down to finishing their dinner, relishing each delicate morsel in between sips of tea. They ate without exchanging a word. Despite being engrossed with his meal, the prince had the strange feeling that they were being watched. It was an extra sense he was perhaps born with, honed through countless hours of hunting. It came into play when he combed the forest for prey, but this time it felt different—he realized that the rapid beat of his heart was due to fear not excitement. He had the uncanny feeling that he was the one being stalked by a predator greater than himself. He calmly placed his tea cup on the table. Then he held his breath and slowly turned his head to look at the small round window on the far wall. Even though he had steeled himself for the unexpected, he was startled to see a face with pitch-black eyes staring at him! He yelled in fright and jumped to his feet, sending the plates clattering on the table. His friends jumped to their feet as well, upturning the low table and causing the plates and cups to crash to the wooden floor while the maid shrieked in alarm!

Not one to stand on ceremony, Raja Perita impulsively jumped down the steps and dashed out of the room, followed closely by Yala and Satra. He passed the startled owner on his way out. The perplexed man started to protest, 'Who will pay for the . . .' but realized that the prince was no longer in the teahouse. He was left standing by himself, looking slightly foolish. Fortunately, before catching up with the others, Chula had decided to stay behind to calm the agitated teahouse owner and pay him for the splendid dinner and tea.

The Ruined Temple

The prince ran to the back of the teahouse but the alleyway appeared to be empty. He paused and scanned the place with narrowed eyes; even in the dark he was able to make out the patterns on the window shutters—there was a mouse scampering on one of the window sill. Finally, he noticed a mysterious figure, half hidden in the dark shadows at the end of the alleyway. By now, his friends had managed to locate him. They drew abreast, slightly out of breath. He said to them, underneath his breath, 'There is a shadow trying to flee . . . perhaps we will hunt tonight!' His eyes were animated, a predator on the scent of prey. The wayward prince had already decided to pursue the strange figure.

Satra said apprehensively, 'Be careful, my lord! It is the night of the blood moon . . . ghostly beings may be roaming the night.'

At that moment, they all heard an owl call out, an eerie and chilling hoot. Chula felt the hair on the nape of his neck stand on end. He said apprehensively, 'An owl's call is a harbinger of misfortune . . . my lord, Perita, we should return home at once!'

Yala said sardonically, 'Save your breath, Chula. You know that the prince is not about to give up a good chase just because an owl hooted.'

He was right, Raja Perita was too intent on his quarry to pay any attention to either Satra or Chula. He had already taken off in hot pursuit of the fleeing figure. When he came in sight of the mysterious figure, he called out in the most persuasive voice he could muster, 'Wait . . . I just want to talk to you!'

The figure was that of a woman. She turned to look at him. In the light of the moon he was able to make out her pale face and dark eyes. She looked oddly familiar but he could not place her . . . Then her lips twisted into a mocking smile, she was taunting him. The woman made an unexpected turn in another alley and ran among the trees close to the edge of town. He did not realize that his companions were no longer with him.

The prince ran heedlessly towards the trees and unexpectedly came to a clearing at the edge of the forest. He was surprised to see a ruined edifice in the middle of the clearing; it was the remains of what was once a magnificent temple. The stone ruin glowed eerily in the light of the red moon. The prince was startled; he knew every nook and cranny of Kota Aur, but he had never come across this place before. The prince hesitated for an instant; then he made up his mind and walked resolutely into the ruins of the ghostly temple. He walked up a flight of massive stone steps into the courtyard of the temple.

The air was infused with the fragrance of flowers. The prince recognized the heavy scent, Champaka flowers in full bloom. It was overpoweringly sweet, sensuous and opulent with an undernote of decay. Raja Perita looked around him and realized that the temple was ringed with the trees; he felt slightly dizzy and sick after breathing in the perfumed air.

He was about to call out to his companions when he heard a silvery laughter and a woman slowly materialized out of the shadows. The pale light of the moon caught her face; she was hauntingly beautiful with skin the colour of rich dark honey. He was reminded of the term *hitam-manis*, sweet-black. Long black wavy hair cascaded down her back. He wondered if she was the same woman he had been pursuing . . . No, he thought, the other woman had been pale and wan . . . and had straight hair.

She looked young too, he guessed that she was probably the same age as he was. Her clothes and body were richly ornamented, worthy of a queen no less. Swathed in a scarlet silk and gold brocaded cloth, heavy gold earrings hung on her delicate earlobes and ornate jewels encircled her neck and wrists. The diamonds and rubies which encrusted her jewels glinted in the moonlight. Her dusky skin and finely chiselled features reminded him of the sailors from that ancient land to the West: Bharat. But he had never seen a woman from Bharat, all the sailors were men. He had also heard that the sailors from Bharat never allowed women on board their ships—it was considered extreme bad luck. So how did she come to be here, all alone in a deserted temple in the outskirts of Kota Aur?

He was intrigued, was she really from that faraway land? Then their eyes met and he was riveted. He could not take his eyes away from her glittering dark ones and those exquisitely curved blood red lips. His pulse quickened even more. He wondered, was it fear he felt or excitement?

The dark beauty smiled and walked slowly towards him, her movements so graceful that she seemed to be walking on air. She whispered, 'A beautiful young man running astray in the middle of the night . . . does your mother know that you're here?'

The hint of cruelty in her voice somehow broke the spell. He forced himself to look away from her eyes and retorted sharply, 'I don't need my mother's permission . . . anyway you're no older than I am! Who are you? Why are you alone out here?'

She laughed again, perfect white teeth flashing in the moonlight. When she spoke her voice was silvery and seductive, almost a whisper, 'I am the keeper of this temple . . . and I am always alone.'

She floated towards him, almost imperceptibly, but his keen senses noticed her movement and he drew back. He snapped, 'Stay away from me . . . my friends are near!'

The strange woman said playfully, 'Surely you are not going to call for help, my lord? Are you afraid of being all alone with me, little prince?'

By now his heart was pounding uncomfortably but he suppressed his mounting fear. He was too fascinated by this strange creature. 'Why would I fear a mere woman? And how do you know about me?' retorted Raja Perita.

The woman threw back her beautiful head and laughed out loud. A rippling laughter which echoed through the ruins. She said, 'Who has not heard of the wild princeling? I can hear your heart beating even from here. Why, you are truly fearful, my lord!'

Raja Perita replied with as much contempt as he could muster, 'You presume too much, strange woman! I am merely concerned!'

And to show that he had no fear for her, he lunged at her and grasped her wrist roughly in his strong hand. She allowed him to pull her close to him and placed her delicate bejewelled hands on his face to take a closer look at him. Her forwardness surprised him but he was even more surprised by how cold her hands were. But it was her eyes which chilled him, dark, cold and ancient, eyes tormented with pain and suffering and not quite sane. He wanted to pull away but somehow his limbs refused to obey him.

He heard her murmuring, 'So strong and full of life . . . it must be wonderful to be so young and so alive! I can even feel the warm blood coursing through your veins underneath your skin.'

The startled prince snapped, 'What is wrong with you, woman? Why are you talking to me like that? Of course I'm alive!' He gathered his strength and with a supreme effort of will pushed her away; he was disconcerted at how much effort it took to push away someone so slender.

The woman laughed mockingly, but this time her silvery laughter sounded menacing not seductive. It dawned on the prince that she was not in the least bit shy or afraid of him, as most young maidens in Kota Aur were. She said,

'It has been a long time since I fed on the blood of a royal prince! The blood prince of Langkasuka.'

The prince decided he could no longer pretend to be unafraid. He drew out his dagger, an ornate weapon with an ivory hilt and a curved blade, but it was a little too late. Her smile widened and twisted into a hideous snarl and she pounced on him. He managed to strike her but she moved with such speed that the sharp pointed tip of the dagger only just managed to trace a line across one cheek. Her face showed shock and disbelief as the thin line turned red and blood oozed out. She gasped out, 'How did you break my spell . . . no one has been able to do that for centuries.' Then the dark woman moved with incomprehensible speed and gripped his arms with superhuman strength and snarled, 'There may be more to you than meets the eye, arrogant cur, but I can overpower any man.'

The prince felt iron hard nails digging into his flesh. It was even more terrifying when she opened her mouth. He saw that she had long sharp pointed fangs which glinted in the moonlight. For the first time in his life, the prince knew true fear. He broke out into a cold sweat and, with his heart pounding, tried to break free from her grip but it was futile. In the struggle, a drop of blood from her cheek fell on his lips. The fangs sank into his neck; Raja Perita cried out, he felt cold gripping him like a vice and all the warmth in his body draining away with his blood. He had never thought it possible to feel so cold before darkness enveloped him.

When his friends finally located him, they found him lying on the ground with a dark figure crouching over him. Yala, who was the first to reach the scene, yelled out, 'The prince is down!' and rushed towards the dark figure. The creature sprang to its feet and fled. Yala drew his dagger and gave chase but the figure seemed to melt away into the shadows.

'What was that hideous thing?' Satra asked as he tried to revive the prince. Raja Perita was hardly conscious and his neck was covered with blood.

'Probably a blood-sucking demon! It's a good thing we found the prince so quickly,' Chula replied.

Satra felt fear gripping him when he realized that the prince could bleed to death. He called out, 'Yala! Where are you? We have to take the prince back to the palace now!'

Yala re-joined his friends; he was out of breath. He gasped, 'I couldn't catch her, she was almost flying.'

The young men carried the prince all the way to the palace as quickly as they could. They placed Raja Perita on his bed, a raised wooden platform at one end of his chamber. It was covered with several layers of cotton and silk beddings. The prince was deathly pale and seemed barely alive.

The queen tended his wounds with whatever skills she had but the bite on his neck refused to heal. She whispered to him, 'Live my son, live! Don't give in to death.'

Her tears fell on his face, but Raja Perita was too delirious to notice. Satra, who had stayed behind to tend to the prince, was sitting crossed-legged on the mat some distance away. He was surprised by how closely the prince resembled his mother. Both had a hairline which formed a widow's peak on their forehead and sweeping feathered eyebrows which framed their eyes—eyes of burnt umber. But the queen had a streak of silvery hair which sprang in the midst of her raven black tresses all the way down her back.

He heard her speak to the unconscious prince, 'My son, my only child . . . I need you to live. Please do not leave me. I cannot bear to lose you; you have to live.'

Satra had never seen the queen looking so distraught; she was the most self-possessed woman he had ever met and he had sometimes believed that she was incapable of emotions. She was not cruel or unkind either, she just seemed remote. He was even more surprised when she started to cry. Her sobs racked her body. Had he been conscious, the prince would have been surprised as well because his mother rarely showed him any overt expressions of affection.

Satra was even more surprised when he noticed that the tears which spilled on Raja Perita's neck seemed to heal his wounds; the blood flow from his neck was slowly being stemmed by the queen's tears. Satra murmured to himself, 'Perhaps the rumours of her faerie blood are true.'

Meanwhile, Tok Dukun, a healer who was skilled in both medicine and magic, had been summoned to treat the prince. When he arrived, the queen implored him, in a voice trembling with fear, 'Tok Dukun, please heal my son. He came home bleeding from a terrible wound on his neck. I've managed to stem the blood flow but he is so weak. I'm not sure if he will survive.'

Satra explained to him, 'The prince came upon an abandoned temple on the outskirts of Kota Aur . . . and there was a strange vicious woman lurking there who attacked him, Tok Dukun. She bit his neck, like a wild beast! We all saw her, I swear it on my life.'

Tok Dukun looked grave. He was a middle-aged kind-looking man, gentle in manner and speech, but with an air of confidence. He got to work without a word. He examined the wound and was relieved to see that the blood flow had been stemmed. He took out an earthenware container from his pouch, opened it and carefully applied a special salve made from sandalwood paste, the pounded bark of cinnamon, essential oil from *lengkuas* leaves and leaf poultice from *akar siak* on to the wound. The salve dried up the gashes on his neck and completely sealed the wound, protecting it from infection. All this time, he was reciting an incantation softly.

When the prince regained consciousness, Tok Dukun helped him to sit up and gave him a potion which contained among other things, liquid extracted from the boiled roots of *penawar pahit* mixed with the pounded fruit of the *Melaka* tree and blended with finely shredded *pegaga* leaves. The prince was persuaded to drink the bitter concoction to take away his pain and restore his strength. Raja Perita fell into a deep sleep but he was breathing normally.

When he was sure the prince was out of danger, Tok Dukun explained to the queen, 'My lady, we are truly fortunate that the wound inflicted on the prince had healed partially by the time I arrived. He has tremendous *semangat*. My lady, I believe that Raja Perita was attacked by a blood-sucking demon, perhaps a *pontianak*.'

The queen frowned when she heard the word *pontianak*—women who died in childbirth were thought to turn into blood-sucking demons called *pontianak*. She was silent for a while. Finally she said, 'Are you sure about this, Tok Dukun? From everything I've heard, *pontianak* usually attack other women, especially those about to give birth. I feel this is something quite different.'

Tok Dukun said, 'I've heard that a *pontianak* sometimes attack men as well, my lady, especially if she has been wronged by a man.' He paused and added, 'In any case, you may be right, my lady. It could be another type of *puaka*. I am, after all, only a humble Tok Dukun; my skill lies in making healing potions, salves and simple charms to treat illnesses of the body and spirit and the occasional mending of broken bones. I have no knowledge of dark magic.'

Before taking his leave, he advised the queen, 'When the prince is stronger, you may want to invite Tok Pawang, to a special healing ritual; she is a spirit medium who has knowledge of dark magic and they say she even has control over animal spirits.'

The queen nodded silently. Tok Pawang was the powerful shaman of Bujang Valley. Everyone feared and respected this formidable woman and no one would dream of crossing her. Their paths crossed every year during the ritual summoning of the rice spirit, but the queen found the stern, hard-faced woman with the impenetrable dark eyes, unnerving. She preferred to rely on Tok Dukun, who had a vast knowledge of plants and herbs, and a proven ability in healing.

Tok Dukun visited the prince every day to administer his potions and massage his limbs to make sure that the muscles in his limbs did not waste away. It took many days for Raja Perita to recover; his body was racked with pain and the people in the palace shuddered to hear his screams at night as nightmares sank their claws into him. His friends took turns to stay by his side at night. He had grown pale and drawn as he frequently refused to eat the food prepared for him. His mother visited him every day, just before nightfall. When he was well enough, she asked him, 'My dear son, why must you risk your life and venture into such dark places?'

His voice was a whisper, 'I'm sorry to have caused you so much disquiet, Mother, but I find joy in dark places.'

She sighed and said, 'Surely there is joy to be found among family and friends, and everyday life? I suppose it is pointless for me to ask you to promise never to put yourself in such danger again?'

He replied in a voice laden with irony, 'You mean should I find the strength to leave my room, ever again, Mother?'

The queen felt her heart grow cold with dread on hearing his words. After this brush with death, the prince could barely walk out of his room without gasping for breath. The queen quelled her own fear—that he would never be able to ascend the throne and fulfil his role as ruler of Langkasuka—and replied with all the conviction she could gather, 'Do not doubt yourself, my dear son. I am sure that you will recover your life force again one day. Meanwhile, we will do all we can to search for a cure for your ailment.'

The Cook's Tale

Late one evening, on a night of the full moon, exactly a month after his terrifying encounter with the dark woman, Raja Perita felt unexpectedly hungry. He sat up in bed and asked for his favourite dish—*gulai bayam*—spinach cooked in coconut milk and rice broth. Satra, whose turn it was to sit with him, was surprised but pleased. He got up immediately and rushed to the royal kitchen, which was housed in a separate annex to the main palace.

This was normally the duty of his man servant but Satra decided that he would be able to accomplish the task faster. He burst into the kitchen and announced, 'Cook, you have work to do! Raja Perita is craving for his favourite dish!'

The cook was surprised to see Satra—dinner had already been served, the dishes washed and she was getting ready to rest for the night. She almost never cooked after sunset, unless it was an emergency. Furthermore, the kitchen depended on natural light from the large bay windows; apart from the fading light from the setting sun, the only other light source was the hearth and a small oil lamp.

But she got up with alacrity and stoked the hearth with more firewood. She was a stout woman with extremely strong hands; able to wield a heavy chopper with ease and slice a large joint of meat with a single blow. And she seemed impervious to pain; once her four assistants—the offspring of relatives—were shocked to see her pick up a piece of fish frying in a pan with her bare hand! But her strong hands were also able to create delicately spiced dishes and sweets, and carve flowers out of fruits such as papaya and mangoes.

The cook was the seventh generation in a long line of royal cooks. In fact, her ancestors had been cooking for the rulers of Langkasuka since the beginning of the dynasty, centuries ago. Recipes for the creation of favourite royal dishes were closely guarded secrets and passed down from father to son or sometimes to daughters. The family also inherited the knowledge of herbs and rare spices—cardamom, cloves and cinnamon from Bharat; pepper and nutmeg from the Moluccas; and tea and garlic from the Tang kingdom. The cook also maintained a large kitchen garden where she grew local herbs and spices: galangal, turmeric, *serai* or lemongrass, *pandan* leaves, the wickedly hot *chilli padi* and vegetables such as *bayam*, a variety of spinach, and *pegaga*.

Most importantly, she knew the best way to combine them to obtain the best flavours for a wide variety of meat, vegetable and seafood dishes as well as an array of tempting desserts. Her family also knew the merchants from the Spice Islands and from Bharat who were the purveyors of these spices and were careful to cultivate their acquaintances through the generations. She had been chosen to be the royal cook because she had 'the touch'—her sense of smell and taste was matchless among all her siblings and cousins.

When the fire was alight, the cook placed a small earthenware pot on the hearth and ladled some diluted coconut milk into it. She chopped the *bayam* leaves and some fresh ginger and turmeric. When the coconut milk in the pot started to boil, she added the rice—fragrant wild rice with reddish-brown skin. This was followed by the spinach, ginger and turmeric. Then salt was carefully added while Satra patiently waited outside the kitchen.

Finally, when the rice was cooked, she ladled the broth into a fine silver bowl and proceeded to garnish it with herbs—a handful of nutritious *pegaga* leaves and some coriander leaves for fragrance. However, while slicing the coriander leaves with a small knife over the bowl, she accidently cut her forefinger. Years of cooking had made her hands insensitive to pain but the cut was deep enough to make her drop the knife which hit the floor and flew under a shelf. The cook bent down to pick it up. As her back was turned, she did not see the sticky red liquid which dripped down the floorboards from the ceiling into the steaming broth.

She jumped when she heard him call out, 'Cook, we haven't got all night! Remember the prince is hungry!'

She was puzzled when she saw how dark the broth in the bowl had turned; perhaps she had used the red variety of *bayam* without realizing it. In any case, there was no more time to make fresh broth and she had used up the last of the *bayam*. She looked around to see if Satra had seen anything amiss but he was standing out of sight. Still puzzled, she placed the bowl of broth on a silver tray and handed it to Satra.

When she bent down to pick up the pot to wash it, she felt drops of liquid fall on her hair and clothes. She looked up at the wooden ceiling and saw the dark stain. A few drops fell on her face. The cook rubbed the liquid with her fingers and knew at once that it was blood. She felt faint; she knew why the broth had turned so dark, she had served broth tainted with blood to the prince. Without a word, she ran to her quarters outside the royal kitchen to wash herself and rest for the night. She couldn't cope with this tonight.

Satra carried the tray carefully all the way to Raja Perita's bedchamber and placed it before him.

Raja Perita finished every drop of the bowl of spinach and rice broth. The prince commented, 'There was something different about the broth today, Satra . . . it was really delicious! I wonder what extra ingredient was added to it.'

The next morning, Raja Perita told everyone that he felt much better. He even got out of bed to go for a walk outside the palace; something he had not done since that fateful night.

When his mother asked him what had made him feel so much better, he replied, 'I think it was the *gulai bayam* I was served last night. It was the best dish I've ever tasted in my life.'

His mother realized there was something different about the broth. She summoned the cook and questioned her, 'After many days of poor appetite, the prince ate up all his food yesterday. He stated that there was something different about the *gulai bayam* yesterday. I need to know what you added to the broth to make it different.'

The cook maintained steadfastly that she had prepared the rice and spinach as always. She was terrified that she would be punished if the truth came out that she had served tainted food to the prince. She said with a note of desperation in her voice, 'My lady, please believe me. I prepared the *gulai bayam* exactly the way I have always done!'

Finally the queen said in exasperation, 'You are the royal cook and we value your long service to the palace. But if you do not tell me the truth now, not only will you be punished but all the members of your family will be removed from our service!'

The cook, who was on her knees all this time, threw herself on the floor and broke into tears. Above all else, she did not want to be the one to bring disgrace to her family and clan. She stammered, 'Please forgive your unworthy slave, my lady! I swear that I prepared the *gulai bayam* as I have always done!'

The queen looked at the prostrated woman with intense frustration. She felt like slapping her. Then she frowned and realized that perhaps a show of force was not the answer. Perhaps the cook needed to be reassured. She drew in a deep breath and spoke as warmly as she could, 'Listen, cook, I only want to know the truth. Is it possible that an accident took place while you were cooking the *gulai bayam*? Perhaps it was something that you had not even realized at the time. No matter what it is, you have my word that nothing will happen to you or your family if you only tell me the truth.'

The cook sobbed and said in a fearful voice, 'My lady, I am prepared to go to prison but please do not punish my family. Your slave accidently cut her hand while preparing the *bayam* broth last night and, while I was looking for the knife, blood spilled into the prince's soup! Your . . . your slave had no time to prepare more soup so she had to serve the . . . prince . . . the tainted soup.'

The queen gasped. 'You mean you served soup tainted with your blood to the prince?'

The cook corrected herself, 'No, my lady! The blood was dripping down from the roof of the kitchen! It fell into the broth and I never knew until later . . . your slave is so very sorry! She implores you to forgive her, my lady! Your slave promises never to allow this to happen again!'

The queen was stunned to hear the cook's explanation. She asked incredulously, 'There was blood falling from the roof of the kitchen?'

The cook, 'I swear, I'm telling the truth, my lady. The blood even dripped on to my clothes and my hair.'

The queen was perplexed until she realized something. The cook did not know that there was a room above the kitchen, which sometimes served as a holding room from lower-ranking visitors to the court.

After a long pause, she said, speaking more to herself than the cook, 'Blood . . . so it was human blood, after all.'

The cooked nodded, looking guilty and fearful.

Then the queen spoke more resolutely, 'Then blood it will be. He is my only son and his life must be saved at all cost! Cook, I order you to add some human blood to the prince's food every day from now onwards.'

Although the cook was relieved that she was not to be punished for her mistake, she was horrified by what she was asked to do! Surely the queen was not serious about her request! She stammered, 'But where will we get human blood every day, my lady? I have only four kitchen helpers and we cannot possibly cut ourselves and at the same time prepare food in the kitchen for the rest of the royal court! It takes time for a wound to heal.'

The queen frowned but realized that she had a point, food contaminated by blood would be abhorrent to most of the court! Besides she did not want anyone to know about the prince's need for blood.

After some thought she said, 'Leave this to me. I will arrange for a bowl of blood to be sent to the kitchen every day. The blood is to be added only to the food prepared for the prince.'

The cook replied with a deep bow, 'I hear and obey, my lady.'

Then she turned towards the cook and warned her, 'The prince's strange desire must be kept a secret! I want you to swear that this information must never leave these four walls, on pain of death! Even the prince himself and his three friends must never know the truth.'

The cook gave her solemn word to the queen, 'My lady, I swear on my life that I will never reveal this secret to anyone.'

The queen later summoned the royal chamberlain, Maharaja Lela, to her audience chamber. He was a tall, imposing man with a sallow complexion. He was the son of a Brahmin priest, who had married a noblewoman of Langkasuka. His father had returned home to Bharat when he was still young and his mother had raised him by herself. However, he did not want for anything materially, because she was wealthy in her own right. Contrary to custom, Maharaja Lela always dressed in black, which made him look even paler than he really was. Maharaja Lela somehow managed to strike fear among all the palace retainers and, like the queen, always seemed cold and collected. The two of them ran the palace and settled disputes among the townsfolk and the villagers throughout the kingdom. Their competency spared the king from having to deal with such mundane matters so that he could receive foreign envoys, visiting royalties and also the wealthy merchants from Bharat, the Han Kingdom and Arabia who traded with Langkasuka.

Maharaja Lela bowed ceremoniously. 'How may I assist you, my lady?'

'I believe the cook may know about the horrid incident last night. Or rather she thinks that someone has been stabbed to death on the roof of the kitchen.'

Maharaja Lela raised an eyebrow. 'I see, my lady. That is an inconvenience. I shall have to speak to the cook later about the need for secrecy.'

The queen said hesitantly, 'But that murder may have saved the prince's life . . . some of the blood dripped into the broth which was later served to the prince. As you can see, he finally managed to get out of bed this morning.' She paused, too fearful to continue.

Maharaja Lela waited impassively for the queen to continue. 'I know that I am asking a great favour of you, Maharaja Lela, but the prince has developed a strange illness since he was attacked by that fearful vampire at the temple.'

Maharaja Lela said, 'I live to serve you, my lady. State your command without hesitation.'

The queen continued, 'I believe there are a few prisoners who are awaiting execution. I would like you to ask them, if they are willing to sacrifice a little of their blood every day for the royal kitchen. If they agree, they will not be executed.'

She felt herself cringe, even as the words left her lips. The queen was relieved to see that Maharaja Lela's face was as unperturbed as ever. He replied impassively, 'Forgive me, my lady, but I presume that the blood is for the prince?'

The queen looked slightly discomfited but she quickly concealed the fact and said, 'I confess that it is so. And, my lord, no one must know of this.'

Maharaja Lela bowed low and said, 'I hear and obey, my lady. No one shall learn of this, on pain of death.'

When he had made the arrangements, Maharaja Lela went to see the queen again. His voice was sombre when he told her, 'All the prisoners have agreed to our condition. They were actually pleased at the prospect of being released after a few months for giving some blood instead of being executed.'

The queen nodded and said apprehensively, 'Thank you, my lord. Are you sure no one will find out the truth?'

Maharaja Lela assured her, 'They think the blood is a sacrificial offering which is quite a plausible explanation. There is a Bhairava cult here in Langkasuka itself, which I have been investigating for some months. Rumour has it that they offer blood sacrifices, completely appalling, of course. The only three people who know the true purpose for the blood are: your serene highness, the cook and my humble self.'

The queen nodded. 'And did you find out anything about our unfortunate visitor?'

'Apparently, he came from the Khmer Kingdom. He may have been an informant of ours and I believe he brought back some important information about the Khmer Kingdom. Unfortunately, he was silenced before he could convey the information to the King. It appears that we have an enemy spy within the court of Langkasuka.'

The queen sighed. 'It appears to be so. And the King, how is he?'

Maharaja Lela said impassively, 'My lord is still in seclusion.'

In the coming weeks, the queen was relieved to see that the prince made a complete recovery; within a month he was fully restored to his former strength and vigour. In fact, his wounds had healed so well with not even the faintest trace of a scar, causing Maharaja Lela to suspect a supernatural agent at work.

The Hunt

His eyes flew open and the hair at the back of his neck stood on end. It was still dark in his chamber and he sensed that the sun had not yet risen. He also sensed something amiss—there were intruders in his chamber—shadows silently approaching his bed. He stealthily reached for his dagger, placed in a recess in the wooden wall beside his bed. He gripped the jewelled ivory handle in his hand, turned around and sat up on the bed in one fluid motion. However, before he could do anything else, a startled but familiar voice called out, 'Wait! My lord! Don't you recognize your own friends?' It was Chula. His friends had decided to ambush him in his chamber at the break of dawn.

Satra called out cheerfully, 'Wake up, my lord! The sun is about to rise and we have a surprise in store for you.'

Raja Perita said angrily, 'How dare you! I was still asleep! What do you think you are doing?' but his three friends ignored his protests cheerfully, pulled him out of the bed and told him to dress up. He decided not to waste his energy by protesting and changed into his outdoor clothes. Several minutes later, they strode out of the palace to embark on their favourite activity—hunting. This had been his usual means of escape from the stifling routine and intrigues of palace life in the past. The thrill of the chase also provided solace whenever he was troubled.

The sun was already peering over the horizon, illuminating the sky with a clear rose tint. It was going to be a glorious day with barely a hint of clouds. The trackers and porters were already waiting for them outside the palace, equipped for the journey. They decided to venture east to the edge of the kingdom where the primeval woods were dark and foreboding, untouched by man. The group walked at a brisk pace, through the secluded path which led out of the palace grounds and through the town itself until they were in open country.

They passed a village whose inhabitants were already up and busy in the fields although it was barely light. It was the harvest season and they had to reap the ripened *padi* as quickly as possible before flocks of marauding sparrows wiped out their precious harvests. The men carefully cut off the rice stalks with a short blade set in a piece of wood; it was taboo to use a sickle to harvest rice as such a cruel instrument might injure the rice spirit. The women followed behind the men, carrying a large tray, woven from bamboo, to collect the stalks of rice and carry them to the sheds to be stored. The rice farmers bowed politely to them as the group passed them, before returning to their work. None recognized the prince who was on foot, dressed as a hunter. In fact, all of them were more or less identically dressed. The rice farmers assumed that they were hunters from the palace, heading for the forest for the regular monthly supply of venison.

Satra commented, 'It must be back-breaking, planting and harvesting rice every year . . . makes me feel quite guilty about my comfortable life.'

Chula replied, 'Well, in return for their hard work, we help to keep the peace and protect them from marauders, pirates, foreign invaders and other churlish malefactors. But you are right Satra, we do owe them a huge debt for providing us with rice—they feed the kingdom.'

Yala sniffed and said, 'There is no need to feel sorry for them, really. They are just simple peasants, you know the hoi-polloi. Forcing them to learn to read and write the ancient language as we had to do would be torture; they are doing the work best suited to them.'

Satra shook his head in disbelief, but Raja Perita said with a grin, 'Well, at least you didn't refer to them as slaves and thralls, as you usually do, Yala.'

Chula remarked, 'Anyway, I heard that portends were good this year. The *sembah* to the Rice Spirit, went really well and everyone is expecting a good harvest. We should have plenty of rice until the next season at least.' He was referring to the summoning of the rice spirit which had taken place only three days ago. No rice crop could be harvested without this all-important ritual.

'I wonder if anyone has ever actually seen the rice spirit?' mused Raja Perita.

Satra replied, 'According to Tok Pawang, the rice spirit takes the form of a young maiden. Legend has it that she was sacrificed a long time ago to give her *semangat* to the rice crops.'

Yala said darkly, 'It is always the young maidens who get sacrificed.'

Raja Perita added, 'I guess that's because the young men get sacrificed in the battlefields.'

Before their mood would darken any further, Chula chipped in, 'Cheer up everyone! It's going to be a lovely day and, remember, we are supposed to be having a good time.'

Everyone was in good spirits. Life was returning to normal. However, as the sun rose and they were in open ground, the prince began to feel oppressed by the heat. He complained, 'Why is it so hot? I feel as if my skin is burning under the sun.'

Chula and Satra, who were walking behind him, looked puzzled. Only two hours had passed since sunrise and the air was still cool although the shroud of morning mist which always covered the land around the forest was clearing up. Chula looked at Raja Perita closely and realized that his skin was turning red. He gasped, 'My lord, you're burning up.'

Raja Perita was about to dismiss this suggestion when he felt the skin on his face and hands starting to burn. His friends noticed that the reddish hue on his face was deepening. Chula said urgently to Satra, 'The prince is averse to the sun! Quick, we have to run into the forest for shade!'

The two of them grabbed the prince unceremoniously by his arms and started running towards the forest. By now the prince felt blinded by the sunlight and did not resist his friends. Yala, who was walking ahead of them with the two trackers, looked in surprise as they rushed past him. He called out, 'Chula! What's going on?'

Chula shouted, 'The prince has a fever! We have to carry him into the shade!'

But before they could reach the forest, Raja Perita had collapsed. Satra and Chula caught him before he hit the ground. Yala ran towards them and helped them to carry the prince as quickly as they could into the shade of the trees. They had to carry him as he was a prince of the blood, no commoner was allowed to touch him except in the direst of situations. One of the porters threw a mat on the ground and the three friends placed the prince on the mat.

Satra remarked in alarm, 'The skin on his face and arms are burnt! Look how red he is—it is as if he came into contact with fire.' He was deeply shocked. He had only seen sunburned skin like this in sailors who had been at sea for a long time.

Yala said, 'Well, we might as well take a break and wait for the prince to recover.'

Chula nodded in agreement. He stood up, turned towards the royal huntsman and said, 'Huntsman, we have to perform the *sembah* to appease the Penungu Rimba.'

The tall, lean stern-faced huntsman bowed slightly towards Chula and said, 'Of course, Lord Chula, as always.'

Chula and the huntsman were familiar with the ritual, having performed it each time they went hunting. They had to ask the permission of the Penungu Rimba, the tutelary guardian of the forest, before they intruded into his domain and harvested its plants and animals. Legend has it that the Penungu Rimba was once a mighty hunter himself who lost his way in the forest and died in its arms. His spirit became bound to the forest he loved so much in life and he became its guardian.

Chula and the huntsman walked a short distance into the trees and held up their arms. They said aloud, 'Datu, forgive our intrusion into your domain and for disturbing your rest. Please allow your servants to pass through and give us permission to harvest a little of your endless bounty.'

When Chula returned, the prince had recovered consciousness. He opened his eyes, dark and sunken with pain, and forced himself to sit up. He said brusquely, 'What are you all doing, standing around me? We can't return home empty-handed! Come—we have a game to catch.'

Satra did not bother to protest, knowing that it would be futile. He helped the prince to his feet, and the four of them together with the two trackers ventured deeper into the forest. The porters remained behind to set up camp. It was cool and misty in the heart of the forest. There were very tall trees with pale white orchids hanging down from the branches. Wild ginger plants bearing flowers in vivid shades of orange and crimson grew on the ground. They walked slowly in the dim light under the arching canopy until a deer darted in front of them! The hunting party gave chase, with the prince far ahead. Finally, the deer disappeared behind a clump of bamboo and the prince realized that he was alone and lost. He thought to himself, 'How can I be lost? I am Perita Deria . . . more at home in the forest than in the palace.'

A slight breeze made the bamboo leaves rustle and the prince felt a strange feeling sweeping over him, an odd mixture of elation and melancholy. The rustle of the bamboo leaves sounded like a voice whispering his name, calling to him from a distance. He walked towards the bamboo stand and entered the grove. The sunlight which filtered through the tall stands of bamboo created shifting patterns of light and shadow on the forest floor. His initial apprehension about being exposed to sunlight vanished; the prince was surprised to find that here the sunlight did not burn him. Hidden at the very centre of the grove was a little forest pool, the colour of a deep green gem. It was fed by a small waterfall, gushing out crystal clear water. Raja Perita felt uplifted as if waves of energy were washing over him; he wondered if it was because of the green light which seemed to suffuse the grove. He decided to sit on the ground and leaned against one of the bamboo trees.

When he looked up, he was surprised to see that there was a woman bathing in the pool—her back was towards him and she was washing her long hair under the waterfall. It was the most extraordinary hair he had ever seen as it fell down her back like a cascade of polished silver. At first he wondered if she was aged because of her silver white hair but her elegant arms, the sensuous curve of her back and her slender waist told him that she was young and beautiful beyond imagination.

Raja Perita sat up in alarm when a young man suddenly stumbled upon the scene, right in front of him. But the young man did not seem to be aware of the prince; in fact, both the young man and the woman in the pool seemed oblivious of his presence. It dawned on the prince that they could not see him, and that he may be having a vision. He leaned back against a tree and watched the unfolding scene, as if he was in a waking dream . . .

* * *

The young man was intent on watching the young woman bathing in the pool. Mesmerized, it never occurred to him to wonder why a young maiden would be bathing by herself in a pool deep in the woods—a young woman with silver hair and skin the colour of ivory. He did not move at all until she seemed to sense his presence, turned and saw him. Her dark eyes registered surprise but it was only momentary; she smiled at him without a trace of alarm or shyness. The young man called out to her, 'Fair maiden, do not be afraid of me! I am not a brigand or a demon and I mean you no harm! Please do not run away!'

The vision of loveliness burst out laughing, her laughter echoing around the grove. 'You don't have to beg, young man! But what an unexpected surprise, I never expected a prince to honour me with a visit.'

He was too stunned to say anything. She walked slowly in the water towards the water's edge and held out her hand to him, 'Why don't you join me in the pool, my lord, Srikanta? You're covered in sweat and grime.'

And the bewitched young prince did enter the forest pool, not quite aware of what he was doing. The coldness of the water revived him somewhat and he was able to stammer, 'Who are you? How do you know my name?'

The strange maiden laughed again, obviously amused. She said, 'I am the faerie of this forest grove and the forest speaks to me! The trees and the animals have been whispering to me about a young prince from a faraway land, who is hunting in my forest without my permission.'

Srikanta apologized humbly, 'Please forgive me, I did not know that the forest belonged to anyone. But I have lost my heart to you, faerie maiden. Will you come with me to my palace across the seas?'

The faerie seemed to have a change of heart. She turned away and said, 'My life is tied to this place and I will perish if I am away from the grove for too long,' and she started to move away from him.

But the young man pulled her by her arms towards him and tried to kiss her blood-red lips. The strange maiden pushed him away and warned him, 'My prince, I am not just a faerie but a faerie who is cursed! Anyone who touches me will be tainted by the curse which I carry.' Her voice was unexpectedly sombre, she was no longer flirting with him.

The young man replied without a moment's hesitation, 'I find it hard to believe anyone so beautiful could be cursed. Do not push me away, I am willing to take the risk of incurring this strange curse of yours.'

She turned around to face him. Her dark eyes were alluring when she smiled and placed one hand on his shoulder while the other caressed his dark hair. When her hand touched his hair, every strand of his jet-black hair turned silvery white. But he was not aware of what was happening to him. She said, 'Very well, Raja Srikanta, come to me then.'

When Srikanta woke up he found himself lying, cold and shivering, on the banks of the stream. When his men found him, he was delirious; at first they could not recognize him as he seemed to have aged several years in the space of a few hours. One of them said in a shocked voice, 'It's the prince all right, but his black hair has turned completely white.'

The leader of the group said, 'It must be some form of dark magic . . . a demon must have swallowed his life force. We have to summon a healer.'

They covered him with a blanket and helped him to make the journey back to the ship.

* * *

When Raja Perita woke up he found himself lying near the banks of the stream. Chula, Yala and Satra were leaning over him, their faces showing a mixture of alarm and concern. They had found him in a state of semi-consciousness. Surprisingly, it was Yala who was the most contrite. He said, 'Please forgive me for putting you in harm's way, my lord! I should have realized it was too soon to take you out hunting, after your ordeal at the temple.'

The prince interjected briskly, 'Spare me your remorse, Yala! You are confusing me. I prefer your thoughtless sarcasm to this display of regret.'

Yala shrugged, he realized the prince did not want to be reminded of his recent disability. He said in an ironic voice, 'Very well, my lord; in any case you seemed to have made a remarkable recovery. Did you find some magical herbs in the forest?'

Raja Perita glared at Yala but Satra intervened, 'He is telling the truth, my lord. The skin on your face and hands have almost healed.'

The prince looked at his hand and realized that he was telling the truth. The skin was still red but the blisters and peeling skin were gone.

Throughout this exchange, Chula had looked concerned. He finally said, 'I sense that this place is *keras*, there is dark energy here. We should head back to camp as soon as possible.'

The rest of them fell silent, they understood what he meant. The air was thick with magical energy; even though it seemed to have helped the prince, they did not know how it would affect the rest of them.

They helped the prince to make the journey back to the camp. Three tents had been set-up and a large welcoming fire lit in the middle of the triangle formed by the tents. The hunters had even brought down a game—a small deer—which the porters had skinned, ready to be roasted. They had also brought some rice, vegetables and condiments with them. After a quick meal, they started the journey back to the palace just after the sun had dipped below the horizon. The prince had recovered sufficiently to make the journey home, unaided.

The prince's servant was waiting for them at the entrance of the palace. He was shocked to see Raja Perita's face and helped him to his chamber, accompanied by Satra. For once, the prince was too tired to direct a scornful remark at his poor servant. After making sure that the prince was comfortable, Satra rushed to the kitchen to awaken the cook. Fortunately, she was still in the kitchen, cleaning up with the help of her eldest niece who was also her assistant. The young woman was tall and stout with a smooth round face, very much like the cook herself.

The cook was startled to see Satra. She said in alarm, 'What brings you to the kitchen at this time of the night, Lord Satra?'

Satra replied with his most disarming smile, 'Sorry to detain you, cook! But we had an unfortunate accident during the hunt the prince is indisposed again.'

The cook asked in a concerned voice, 'How so my lord? What can I do to help?' But even as the words came out of her mouth, she had a sinking feeling that she knew what he wanted.

Satra replied, 'The Queen has asked for your special *gulai bayam*; it seems that you are the only one in the kingdom who can make it to the prince's satisfaction.'

The cook said resignedly, 'Very well, Lord Satra. The Queen's wish is my command.'

The cook instructed her niece to light the hearth and place a small pot, half filled with coconut milk, on the fire while she prepared the necessary ingredients herself. She added the ingredients into the pot when it started to simmer and told her niece, 'You can go now, Chomel, I will handle the rest.'

The young woman understood that her aunt wanted to be alone. She placed her palms together and bowed politely to Satra before leaving the kitchen through the back door.

When they had to work late, she sometimes shared her aunt's quarters at the back of the palace.

When the dish was ready, the cook took the pot away from the hearth. Then she went to look for a small container carefully hidden in a recess in a corner of the kitchen. As she had suspected, the container was empty; she could not stop herself from saying out loud, 'Now where am I going to find some blo . . .?'

She managed to stop herself in time but Satra had caught on to her words; he suddenly looked attentive. He interjected sharply, 'Going to find what, cook?'

The cook tried to brush it off, 'Nothing, Lord Satra! Just an old woman mumbling to herself.'

But Satra was not to be put off so easily. He said insistently, 'Out with it, cook! I've always suspected that there was a secret ingredient in your *gulai bayam*!'

When she was sure that her niece was not within earshot, the cook replied stiffly but politely, 'The ingredient is a secret which I am forbidden to reveal, my lord, Satra!'

'I am the prince's closest friend! How could you conceal a secret from me, cook?' demanded Satra.

The cook looked mortified. She replied with her head bowed, 'I am sorry but this is not my secret to reveal, my lord . . .'

'Oh come on, dear cook, you know I would never break a secret, especially one which could harm our prince,' he tried to sound as persuasive as possible.

'My lord, I have been sworn to secrecy, on pain of death!' she whispered fearfully, looking around her apprehensively to make sure there was no one eavesdropping.

'By whom?' he demanded. Even as he asked this question, it dawned on him that the person in question must be someone in a high enough position to be unassailable. Who could be heartless enough to threaten the life of our beloved cook? More to the point, what secret would be worth her life?

'I can't even reveal to you the name of this person, my lord,' she whispered even more fearfully.

What could it be? He pondered. His initial guess of rhinoceros horn, toad's eyes, snake oil and even the heart of the rare gold sunbird hardly warranted a death sentence. As the awful realization dawned on him, Satra said abruptly, 'It's blood isn't it? The secret ingredient in your *gulai bayam* is human blood!'

The cook gasped out loud, and covered her mouth with her hands. Finally she said, 'How did you know? I never told anyone . . . no one is supposed to know.'

Satra interrupted her, 'Cook, I am neither blind nor foolish, although Yala would have it otherwise. We all know that the prince's affliction is supernatural in origin, and I have been observing you and the prince for the last few months. I draw my own conclusions and what you told me about having to keep a secret on pain of death, just confirmed it.'

The cook said in a fearful voice, 'Lord Satra, please do not tell anyone. I have been sworn to secrecy and I do not want to die! No one must know of this.'

Satra reassured, 'You have my word, cook, that no one will hear of this . . . At least not from me. But where do you intend to obtain blood, at this time of night?'

The cook wiped her hands on a piece of cloth and said in a resigned voice, 'We draw blood from the prisoners, but it will have to be my blood, seeing as Maharaja Lela has retired for the night.'

'No, cook. I can't expect you to make such a sacrifice,' and Satra drew out his dagger and was about to make a small cut on his hand when the cook stopped him.

'Wait! Don't use your hunting knife, you will wound yourself unnecessarily! Use this instead . . . it's much safer . . . and less painful,' and she took out a small implement which was hidden in the recess together with the container for blood. It was a hook, with a very fine sharp pointed end. The cook heated the tip in the fire and explained, 'The sailors from Arabia and Bharat said that the best way to clean a metal object is to heat it in fire.'

'Here, allow me . . . you may do more harm to yourself,' and the cook grasped his left wrist and pierced a tiny blood vessel. Satra winced but it was actually less painful than he had envisaged. Blood oozed out and she allowed the blood to flow into the dish.

When she felt it was more than enough, she quickly pressed the wound firmly with her thumb to stop the bleeding. She asked him to press the wound with his finger while she fetched another small bottle of clear liquid from the recess together with a strip of clean cotton cloth. The cook poured a little of the liquid on the wound and Satra gasped with pain.

He protested, 'This liquid burns! The sting from this liquid is even more painful than the sharp hook! I only offered to give a little blood . . . not to be punished like this.'

The cook muttered, 'Men are such girls . . . the liquid is *arak*, Lord Satra. The strongest form of *arak* there is . . . I get them from the sailors from Arabia. They clean the wound and stop it from festering.'

When she was sure that the wound was clean, she wrapped the strip of cloth firmly around the wound. 'Here, you're all better now. Keep the wound dry for a few days; it's better that you don't take a bath or swim for a week,' she added.

The Bamboo Princess

The queen was horrified to see the burnt skin on her son's face and hands. She questioned the prince, 'How did this happen, my son? Did you get burnt by fire in the forest?'

'No mother. I never came near any fire. It appears that I've developed an acute aversion to sunlight,' he replied in an offhand manner.

She gasped, 'Sunlight? You were burnt by the sun? How is this possible?'

'Apparently, it's another curse the female demon of the forest grove may have inflicted upon me,' he answered resignedly, trying to conceal his frustration.

The queen said in a low voice, 'I'm so sorry that you are burdened with yet another affliction, my dear son.'

The prince replied with a shrug, 'Perhaps I had it all along . . . I've always preferred the night to the day anyway.'

He wondered whether he should reveal the strange vision he had in the forest grove to her. His mother stroked his long hair with her fingers and then gasped in shock, the light from the lamp lit the strands of pale gold among his raven black hair. There were already several strands of pale gold hair growing through the centre parting but much fewer than hers, and they had been hidden among his thick hair.

She gasped, 'You saw her! The cursed one with silver hair . . . did you see the man with her? Did she reveal his name in your vision?'

Taken by surprise, he replied hesitantly, 'Umm . . . it was Raja Srikanta, I think.' He added, in surprise, 'How did you know, Mother?'

Before replying she turned to Bujang and asked him to leave the room. The young man bowed gracefully and walked out of the room slowly, backwards. When she was sure he was out of hearing, she turned to the prince and said, 'There are certain signs that you have been touched by magic . . . please tell me exactly what you saw in the bamboo grove.'

The prince recounted to her his vision in the bamboo forest.

The queen was silent for a long while. She clenched her hand, her face looking troubled before continuing, 'You should not have seen such a vision . . . how could she have subjected you to this?' Then she added with a deep sigh, 'I'm so sorry, Perita. You are the victim here; I hope you were not upset by what you saw.'

Raja Perita raised his voice slightly, 'Mother! I am not a child any more! These things don't upset me.'

His mother gave him a sharp look, and said, 'How would you know, Perita?' Then speaking almost to herself, she said, 'Why must you find darkness everywhere?'

He replied sharply, 'You know very well that it is darkness which finds me, Mother! In any case, I didn't ask to be given this vision! What was she anyway? A faerie?'

His mother covered her face with her hands and said, 'You don't understand, Perita . . . that silver-haired woman was my mother . . . and she was a yakshi.'

The prince looked genuinely shocked momentarily. But he quickly masked it and added darkly, 'So, I know your true origins now, Mother! But isn't a yakshi a forest demon who devours men? I've heard stories that they eat the poor souls who get lost in the forest, leaving behind only their teeth, nails and hair.'

The queen could not help but smile at what she heard. She replied, 'The stories you've heard about the yakshas and yakshis are somewhat exaggerated, my dear Perita. The yakshas are forest sprites; tied to the trees and the streams in the forest and the earth. They are not as benign as the *vidhyadharas* as they have the ability to swallow the life-force of living beings but they do not actually eat people . . . or animals for that matter.'

Raja Perita said, 'That's a small consolation. At least I know I'm not descended from a line of ferocious man-eating demons.'

His mother ignored what he said. She raised her head and spoke in a determined voice, 'This yakshi may have given birth to me, but she did not raise me. My true mother was a kind, brave and strong woman. It is time I told you about her . . . she told me this story about how she found me in the bamboo grove, since I learned to talk.'

She added, 'Come, I will share my vision with you. It is a gift of our yaksha blood; a curse sometimes comes with a gift.'

The queen took both his hands in hers and Raja Perita found himself in a faraway place atop a hill, bathed in bright sunlight. He looked around the place in wonder, basking in the bright sunlight and admiring the view of the forested valley below. He was sharing a vision with his mother:

* * *

A tall middle-aged woman with an angular face was picking her way among the dense brushes on the outskirts of the forest. The harsh lines on her face contrasted with her kind eyes. She was not alone; a few villagers were following her. They were looking for bamboo shoots—tender but crunchy bamboo shoots which were delicious when cooked with fish and coconut milk. The large bamboo stems were also useful for making the floors of huts and for baking delicious sticky *pulut* rice. They walked for quite a distance until they came upon the mysterious forest with towering trees and a profusion of flowers. Inside this forest was a dense grove of bamboo which formed a wall that blocked their way and made it impossible for them to pass through. The tall woman commanded the villagers, 'Cut down some of the bamboo so that we can pass through to the other side! I must find out what is on the other side of the bamboo!'

The woman waited while the villagers swiftly cut down some of the bamboo to create a path for them. When they had cleared the path, the villagers entered the grove; inside, they found a huge bamboo growing in the middle of the grove. It was as thick as a man's thigh and had a large bulge in the middle. It was a *buluh betung*, a giant species of bamboo. The stem of this bamboo was shining gold while its leaves were silver-green in colour. When one of the men tried to cut down the bamboo, milky white sap spilled from the wound and the cut in the stem healed immediately! The villager was alarmed. He rushed to the woman and told her, 'Tok Batin! There is a magical bamboo tree in the forest! When I tried to cut it down, milky white sap flowed from it and the stem healed by itself!'

Tok Batin quickly followed the villager to the site to examine this bewitched bamboo. She took out her machete and whispered a spell over it and cut the bamboo down, just above the bulge. This time the bamboo did not grow back, instead they heard the cry of a child from inside the stem! The surprised woman looked into the hollow stem and saw a tiny baby girl inside! She was the size of a newborn child but had a full head of luxuriant black hair with a streak of silvery hair growing down the middle. The child opened its eyes and looked at her wonderingly and Tok Batin lost her heart to her.

With her heart pounding, she carefully picked the child up with trembling hands and wrapped her in her shoulder cloth. Then holding her high above her head, she exclaimed, 'I have found my long-awaited heir! She has been brought to us as a gift from the faeries!' and took the child home with her.

The child grew up in the village as Tok Batin's daughter and learnt how to cast spells and make charms as well as to cultivate fruit trees such as durians and plantains, and edible roots such as yam and tapioca. Her life was not easy but she was a child who was greatly loved and treated as a treasure by the entire village. Tok Batin named her Putih Jerineh but her people called her Puteri Buluh Betung or Princess Bamboo.

The vision faded and was replaced by another one:

One day a young man sailed into the mouth of a river in a finely constructed perahu; he was accompanied by about a dozen men. He told everyone that he came from a distant land, the youngest son of a raja and as such had no claim to land or property in his own country. He was forced to *merantau*, traverse the archipelago in search of a place to call his own and to seek his fortune. He had arrived at this place as an accident of fate and it appeared to be uninhabited to him. When they landed in a quiet cove, he asked his men, 'This is a fine place to set up our home. Does this place have a name? And does it have a ruler?'

One of the men who served as a guide replied, 'Raja Wangsa, I believe this place is called Jerai. The chief of the land, whom everyone calls Tok Batin, is a woman. According to the people along the coast, she possesses secret power and knowledge, but is of a kind disposition. She lives in the village close to Jerai Hill which is farther upstream.'

His curiosity piqued, Raja Wangsa decided, 'As our *perahu* is too large to travel upstream, let us journey on foot inland, to meet this Tok Batin! Perhaps I can move her kind disposition to allow us to stay here, in the Jerai valley. Who knows? Perhaps this Tok Batin has a comely jungle maiden in her household as well!'

Before the guide could reply, Raja Wangsa issued the following order, 'Six of you will stay with the *perahu* to make sure that it is safe and secure! The rest of you will follow me! And bring along some supplies for the journey.'

The men set off on foot on the long journey to Jerai Hill. Apart from some food, mats and extra clothes they also carried salt, nutmeg, areca nuts, cloves and woven cloth with them. Raja Wangsa was young but he was not a fool and he knew gifts could be extremely useful in bargaining for many things including land!

When they reached Jerai Hill, they were received hospitably by Tok Batin and the rest of the village elders. Raja Wangsa and his men were invited to a simple meal during which time he took the opportunity to request that he and his men be allowed to settle in Jerai. Tok Batin nodded but did not give an answer immediately. Once the meal was over, Raja Wangsa presented gifts to all the elders in appreciation for their hospitality. Not surprisingly, Tok Batin and the delighted elders readily agreed to allow the strangers to settle in the lower reaches of the river, on the condition that 'they did not attempt to settle on land above the white sands'.

To conclude the deal in the time-honoured tradition, the men were offered *sirih* or betel leaf quid by young village maidens. One of them was the Tok Batin's beautiful daughter, the Bamboo Princess. Raja Wangsa was smitten by this 'comely jungle maiden' who was, in fact, a ravishing beauty. He had no doubt that she would have outshone all the proud high-born ladies in his father's palace. The only flaw he could see in her, if it could be called that, was a streak of silvery hair which ran down her head, right in the midst of her raven black tresses.

The maiden prepared a fresh betel quid for him, but, in the process, accidentally cut her little finger with a knife. Raja Wangsa, who was watching her with rapt attention, was stunned to see white blood flowing from the tiny cut! He also recollected the old legends that maidens who bled white blood were descended from faeries and was even more determined than ever to marry her.

Throwing caution to the wind, the young man blurted out, 'My most esteemed Tok Batin, I Raja Wangsa, the son of the Raja of Bujang Valley, would be greatly honoured if you would accept my proposal! Will you allow your daughter to be my wife?'

The young maiden immediately dropped the betel quid she was preparing and coldly walked out of the hut, her head held high. Tok Batin was silent for a while before apologizing for her daughter's action. She explained, 'We are truly honoured by your proposal of marriage, my lord, but it is not for me to decide on such matters. Although I have raised the puteri as my own daughter, she is not my birth child. We found her in a bamboo grove sixteen years ago.'

The old woman smiled gently and continued, 'You have to win her hand and in order to do that, you, Raja Wangsa, have to live here with us and learn our ways.'

The young man weighed his options and decided to live with the orang hulu or hill people. He sent his men away downstream so that they could prepare the land for settlement and build their houses. Raja Wangsa himself lived with the hill' people for twelve full moons and learnt their ways including hunting and harvesting the bounties of the forest. He also learnt how to foretell the weather and changing of the seasons from Tok Batin and from Putih Jerineh, he learnt how to make offerings to appease the forest spirits. In turn he taught the hill people what he knew of the cultivation of crops and the use of spice as condiments.

All the time he was living with them, he was conscious that the Bamboo Princess was watching and appraising him. At first she was cold and aloof and it took him a long time to win her affection and eventually she allowed him to court her. She told him the reason why she had walked out on him when they first met, 'It was not that I did not find you handsome and well spoken; but your presumption in assuming that I would agree to marry any stranger just for some gifts, angered me.'

Finally, after exactly a year, she agreed to marry him. It was a simple but ancient ceremony in which they shared a meal from a large tortoise shell with the Tok Batin and drank a drought from the empty shell of a terrapin. Very soon after the marriage, Puteri Buluh Betong said goodbye to her people and accompanied her husband downstream to the settlement which had been made ready for them by his followers.

Her new life in the valley with Raja Wangsa was blissful. A young girl from the hill people had accompanied them to their new home in the lowland and helped her with the housework. She hated being confined indoors and loved to accompany her husband when he sailed to distant coastal villages on his *perahu*. One day a massive, three-masted *perahu*, arrived at their village and Raja Wangsa recognized it at once—it came from his homeland. The messenger addressed him as 'His serene and radiant grace Raja Seri Mahawangsa, Heir to the Ancient Throne of Langkasuka.'

There was an urgent message—Raja Wangsa was to set sail immediately as his sister, the Queen and ruler of Langkasuka, was on her deathbed. The Queen had never married and did not have an heir to succeed her. It was the first time the Bamboo Princess found out that her husband was in fact Raja Seri Mahawangsa, the heir to the throne of Langkasuka. Raja Wangsa had no choice but to set sail immediately on the *perahu*. The Bamboo Princess accompanied him to Langkasuka, together with her young maid.

* * *

The queen released her son's hands and they were back in the room. The prince asked, 'You sailed here on the ship, with father?'

His mother replied, 'Of course I did . . . otherwise you and I would not be living in the palace of Langkasuka.'

Before they could continue the conversation further, Satra walked into the chamber, carrying a silver tray with a silver bowl of *gulai bayam* and a silver goblet of fresh coconut water. He placed it on a low carved table, beside the bed. The queen decided to retire for the night, and gracefully walked out of the room.

Raja Perita sat up and slowly ate his dinner. His friend watched in fascination as the burns healed themselves right before his eyes—what would have taken days or even weeks was occurring in a matter of minutes. He remained silent until the prince had finished his meal. By then, most of the raw peeling skin had healed. It would take a few more hours but Satra knew that when the prince wakes up the next afternoon, his skin would have healed completely with no sign that he had ever been burnt at all.

When Satra reached forward to pick up the tray, Raja Perita reached forward and caught his bandaged wrist. His eyes narrowed as he demanded sharply, 'Why did you do it? Why would you ever allow yourself to be bled like that?'

Satra winced with pain, he was taken aback. He said out loud, 'How did you know? And will you let go . . . I'm still in pain!'

Raja Perita released his wrist and replied, 'How could I not know? I smell blood on you, even now. The same blood which was in the food.'

Satra examined his bandaged wrist to make sure the wound had not reopened. Then he shrugged and said, 'It was the least I could do . . . I couldn't very well allow the cook to cut herself. And anyway, I've gone through worse. The wound will heal in a couple of days and they say that blood always replenishes itself.'

The prince said with a trace of bitterness, 'For everyone, except me . . . Are you sure you are all right? They say that it is taboo to spill royal blood . . .'

Satra replied, 'The royalty of my blood is so diluted that I doubt it will unleash a curse . . . Anyway, it's odd how you get felled by beautiful women and almost half-roasted by a bit of sunlight . . . but your grip is like iron . . . maybe you need to rebalance your *chakra*.'

Raja Perita glared at him but decided to ignore his friend for a while. Finally he said, 'Are you going to tell the others about my vile habits?'

His friend replied, 'I won't if you don't want me to. I have a feeling they might have guessed already . . . well at least Yala would . . . of course it might be too much for Chula to accept.' He paused and added with a grin, 'You of course owe me a debt.'

Raja Perita put on an expression of mock pain and said, 'And here I thought that you did it out of selfless love and devotion.'

Satra pressed the palms of his hands together in a gesture of mock supplication and replied, 'I may be noble-born but my family is alas, quite poor. It's not easy keeping up with the fabulously rich Yala or the wealthy Chula!'

Raja Perita sat up in bed as if he had come to a decision. He said, 'I think we should meet up with Chula and Yala tomorrow evening. Ask them to come and meet me at the old cottage at the far end of the palace grounds. It's been abandoned for years since we were children.'

The queen returned to her chamber to rest for the night. She sighed in the darkness. She had not told her son the whole truth about his birth to spare him and herself the pain of that memory. It was best left unsaid. She also wondered about his relationship with Satra. Clearly, her son favoured him over his other friends. Was there more to their relations than met the eye? Individuals who were born male, but adopted feminine clothes and manners, were accepted in court as royal dancers and some became keepers of rituals and culture. In her own tribe such individuals were respected as mediators of special rituals to ensure there were no malign intruders from the spirit world, but neither the prince nor his friends displayed any such inclinations, in fact they obviously took pride in their masculine prowess. She sighed and wished the prince would take an interest in the young noble women who sometimes attended court functions, but to date none of them seemed to have caught his fancy. But then he seemed to enjoy the company of young women in the Inns he frequented. Perhaps he had yet to meet his match.

The queen drifted into a restless sleep and her past revisited her, forcing her to relive one of the most painful episodes in her life.

After a few months of blissful married life, the moment they had both dreaded arrived—a three-masted *perahu* loomed over the horizon. When it finally moored in the estuary, a group of men came to shore on a *sampan*. She was not surprised when they announced that they came from the Langkasuka Court, with an urgent message for Raja Wangsa. After a few days of indecision, Raja Wangsa had decided to return to Langkasuka by himself. She had pleaded with him; the proud and beautiful daughter of Tok Batin begged him for a favour for the first time in her life, 'Let me accompany you to your father's home, my lord, Wangsa!'

He replied, 'You are heavy with child and the journey to Langkasuka will be too perilous for you and my unborn child!' But he promised his wife, 'Wait for me here and do not pine for me. You know that I love you; I promise to return before our child is born!'

As they said their farewell, she wept for the first time in her life, her heart heavy with foreboding. Her mother had told her that it was taboo for her to weep and she should only weep in the direst of circumstances. But her tears came unbidden, and they drained her so much, she collapsed. Her maid helped her to her bed. She sighed to herself and thought, 'He does not want his family to know that his wife is a maiden from the forest, an *orang hulu*!'

After more than a month, her husband had still not returned home. She had sat at the window of their house which looked towards the sea, at sunrise every morning and before sunset in the evening, longing to catch a glimpse of a distant *perahu*. Eventually, the rainy season arrived and she knew that he would be delayed even more. It rained incessantly and the river overflowed its banks and threatened to flood the houses in the village, even though they were raised high on stilts. When the water had almost reached the wooden floor of the house, Putih Jerineh told the girl, 'Please gather all the food we have in the house and my jewellery and best clothes and put them in the *sampan*! I think we have to row upstream to our old village to escape this flood!'

The girl did as she was told and helped her mistress into the *sampan* as well. The two of them rowed as hard as they could upstream against the flow of the river. However, an hour later, Putih Jerineh was about to give birth and cried out, 'I feel terrible birth pangs . . . I cannot help you to row the boat. See if you can manage by yourself!'

But she knew the girl was not strong enough and soon they were drifting towards the open sea, pulled by the strong current. The girl cried out in fear, 'What are we to do, my lady? The *sampan* is being pushed into the sea! We will be lost, the sea will swallow us!'

Putih Jerineh reached out for her hand and reassured her, 'Do not fear little sister . . . I know in my heart that we will be safe.'

They drifted along the coast for some time before she was proven right. A magnificent *perahu* appeared from out of nowhere—it had been hidden by a tree-covered promontory! Her heart soared when she saw the three-masted *perahu*, it was the same *perahu* that had taken Lord Wangsa to Langkasuka three months ago. The maid waved frantically at the *perahu* which came slowly to a halt. A sailor climbed down from the vessel on a rope ladder and asked the maid what was wrong. The maid gestured to her mistress. She said, 'This is my lady Putih Jerineh, the wife of my lord, Raja Wangsa, himself.' The sailor bowed and quickly climbed up to the *perahu* again. As Putih Jerineh could no longer stand, a fish net was lowered to carry her on to the *perahu*. The maid and their belongings followed suit. The Bamboo Princess gave birth to her child on the *perahu*.

Her life in the palace of Langkasuka had not been easy. The high-born court ladies resented her and looked down on her. She knew that they referred to her as that 'rough orang ulu woman from the hills' and sometimes even as that 'half-raksasa woman'. However, her remarkable beauty and natural grace shielded her to a certain extent. It was impossible for people to actually believe that she was 'a rough woman' or 'half-raksasa woman', when confronted by the evidence of their own eyes. Her aloofness was an even stronger defence from their spite and venom; she realized that she was no longer the Bamboo Princess, she was now Queen. After several months of snide remarks and rumour-mongering, the court ladies gave up when it became evident that she was impervious to their insults. But they still withheld information from her and she frequently missed important events, although sometimes she preferred it that way. The young girl who accompanied her to the court tried her best to find out what was happening and even tried spying on the other handmaidens but she was also out of her depth.

The king, who was himself busy learning about running his kingdom from his advisors, was oblivious of the struggle his young queen was going through. It was only when the young chamberlain, Maharaja Lela was appointed that the queen finally had an ally in court. He first requested to see her when she had not turned up for a feast given for an important visitor. She was surprised to see the tall man, dressed in black with discrete gold edging on his costume. He was older than her but still young, perhaps in his late twenties. She had not even known the old chamberlain had retired. He bowed and addressed her politely, 'Please forgive this intrusion, your grace. But the court dearly missed your presence last night at the dinner given for the Prince from Angkor. I have come to enquire if you are not feeling well.'

The queen hesitated before replying. The new chamberlain was polite but not condescending, neither did he convey any of the slyness that some of the courtiers had shown when addressing her. He had a calmness and directness about him that impressed her. She decided to tell him the truth. 'I didn't attend the function, because nobody told me about it. And even if I did know about it, I would be at a loss about what to wear and what to do at such an important occasion. I would rather be absent than embarrass the king in front of the entire court.'

Maharaja Lela looked slightly surprised, it was one of the few occasion when he had expressed emotion. After a pause, he said, 'I apologize for my lack of insight and understanding of your situation and for the distress you must have been going through. I will remedy this situation as best as I can and as soon as I can.'

He had realized in that instant what was happening. The noblewomen of the court had effectively isolated the young queen and intentionally kept her out of important events in the hope that she would soon be rendered unnecessary. The very next day, he assigned a new palace 'handmaiden' to the queen. She had, in fact, retired some years ago and was already a mother of two young children, both daughters. But during her time, her knowledge of court etiquette was legendary but more importantly she was a family friend and had been away from court long enough not to be influenced by any of the court ladies. The queen slowly learned the intricacies of court etiquette from the old handmaiden and in a few months was able to hold her own at the most formal of occasions. The irony was not lost on her, she realized that she was going through what her own husband must have gone through that year he had spent among her people in the hills.

Maharaja Lela and the old handmaiden made her queen of the court of Langkasuka, but it was Tok Pawang who showed her, her true calling and the nature of her power. The shaman, made a surprise appearance early one morning, when Raja Perita was seven years old. The palace guards let her in without question, everyone in Langkasuka knew who she was and held her in awe. She was still not quite old, and at the height of her power. Her long dark hair had streaks of grey, and her face was lined but she held herself up straight and did not really need the gnarled walking stick she always carried with her. Her clothes were not luxurious but in good condition. The court always sent her a new set of clothes at the beginning of each planting season and the royal kitchen as well as the villagers sent her food every week.

She requested to see the 'new queen' when she was inside the palace. To her, seven years at Langkasuka still made the queen a newcomer. She was shown into the queen's audience chamber and greeted by the queen's old handmaiden, who asked her to sit down. Tok Pawang refused and said that she preferred to stand. The queen soon made an appearance and took her sit on the small raised dais. She was not surprised that the shaman did not bow down to her. She said, 'Welcome to Kota Aur, Tok. I have heard of you of course. I and the Royal Court are at your disposal.'

'I too have heard of you, my queen. In the beginning we heard that you were the daughter of the Tok Batin of

Jerai Hills. She is someone we hold in high esteem. But it has come to our knowledge recently that you were found in a bamboo patch and may have the blood of the invisible folks. It is your assistance, that I seek, my queen.'

The queen was surprised. 'My mother has always told me that she found me in the stem of a giant bamboo tree; the type known as *buluh betung*. However, I don't know how my birth is of any great consequence. Anyway, how may I help you?'

Tok Pawang replied, 'The rice harvest has been declining for a number of years. We still have enough for Kota Aur and for the villages this season but there is no reserve. If the next crop fails, there will be hunger in the land . . . and it has not rained for weeks. A few of the Bomohs are already talking about giving a blood sacrifice to appease the rice spirit.'

The queen sat up, her body tensed at the word, 'blood sacrifice'. Her normally smooth voice was sharp when she replied, 'How will a blood sacrifice solve anything? The people who come up with such ideas do so because they know they will not be affected. We must not allow this to take place.'

'Indeed, your grace, you may help us to avoid this abhorrent practice. Word has come to us from the priest in the forest that you may in fact be the offspring of a yakshi. These are beings tied to nature, with power over plants and even animals. I believe you may be able to help us to restore fertility back to the land.'

The queen was even more surprised. She had not taken part in any rituals since coming to court. After a few minutes of pondering over the old woman's request, she said, 'If it means avoiding a famine and a blood sacrifice, I will be happy to come down to the fields. Let me know the day and time, Tok.'

Tok Pawang replied, 'The ritual for the planting season will be three days from today. Please come to the main rice fields at sunrise.' Then Tok Pawang bowed her head slightly and walked out of the room.

The queen kept her word and travelled to the village before dawn three days later. While her two handmaidens and two of her guards waited in the village, she descended into the rice fields with Tok Pawang and a few village women. They carried offerings to the rice spirit, laid on woven trays made of *mengkuang* and bamboo. There was a tray of carefully arranged betel leaves, another filled with areca nuts, one with red sugarcane stalks tied in a bundle, one filled with sheaves of rice and one filled with steamed rice, stained a deep yellow with turmeric. The trays were carefully placed around the main *padi* field.

They walked around the field while Tok Pawang recited a long melodious incantation, which the Queen repeated softly to herself, surprised that the words came to her so easily. The queen sensed that the shaman had real power, she felt herself draw energy from the surrounding, from the breeze and the sunlight and the very air. Her very skin and hair tingled from this energy and, guided by the spell, allowed her to direct this energy to the growing plants in the rice fields. It was something she never knew that she could do. It was late morning when she left and she heard Tok Pawang instruct the villages to secure their farm animals and livestock in the evening. The wealthy had sheds for their animals while poorer people kept them under their house, which was built on stilts.

True enough there was a storm that night, lightning and thunder chasing each other in a circle. But it was a storm which made her feel exhilarated, not an ominous harbinger of misfortune. She sensed that the spell had worked. The rain which followed was heavy but not destructive. Several months later, the rice harvest was one of the most bountiful in years. Livestock and animals were equally fertile, some bearing twins instead of the usual singleton.

The Handmaiden's Tale

The young maiden felt as if she was walking on air; her father had just told her that the queen had agreed to take her on as her personal handmaiden. She was to be given the title of Nong, a minor lady. Her elder sister had served the queen for seven years, after the legendary old handmaiden had retired at the age of fifty and she herself was about to retire from her service at the palace. She was still a young woman of twenty-five, but the queen had given her permission to leave the palace and marry a titled retainer. She was allowed to set up her own household in Kota Aur.

The young maiden was even more beautiful than her elder sister, with large dark expressive eyes, a complexion as smooth and rich as honey and heavy, raven-black hair which reached up to her knees. People described her hair as *mayang mengurai*, the unravelling inflorescence of the areca palm tree. She was also soft spoken and graceful. She would fit in well as a member of the queen's retinue.

Her sister had instructed her carefully about her duties, 'You must always address her as "My Lady". Every sentence addressed to her must begin with, "Forgive me, my lady..."'

'When you enter her chamber, you must kneel, press your palms together and bow your head... And you must never turn your back to her. Always leave with your head bowed and walk backwards... You have to work hard for a few years but you are sure to marry a well-to-do man from the palace.'

One afternoon, while she was combing the queen's hair, Raja Perita entered her chamber unannounced. The handmaiden fell to her knees and lowered her head modestly. The prince burst out, 'Mother! Why can't I go out tonight?'

'My child, Rajaputra Chandra of Sri Vijaya is here with his court and we must do our best to entertain them. In fact, your father, the king, is throwing a grand feast for them tonight and you are required to attend,' the queen replied.

'Surely the king's and your presence is enough to satisfy the mighty Rajaputra of Sri Vijaya! In any case, since when did Langkasuka have to pay homage to Sri Vijaya? Aren't we the more ancient lineage?' the prince protested.

His mother said, 'Alas, Langkasuka is falling on hard times. Some of the ships which came to our port now prefer to trade with Sri Vijaya; the kingdom claimed the right to rule the seas when their first king was gifted with the magical Jewel of Sri Vijaya by the dragon king. They also have the support of the *Orang Laut* and they are quite unassailable!'

Prince Perita had heard of the *Orang Laut*, the sea gypsies, before and said derisively, 'The *Orang Laut* are nothing more than pirates! I've heard that they commandeer ships from the Tang Empire and the Pala Kingdom and force them to trade with Sri Vijaya . . .'

The queen declaimed an old saying, 'Where there is sea, there are pirates, my dear Perita. We should consider ourselves fortunate that Sri Vijaya has chosen to form an alliance with Langkasuka instead of trying to conquer us . . .' She paused and added, 'Sri Vijaya is extremely wealthy and they have gifted us with a *bunga mas*—it is the most extraordinary thing your father and I have ever seen; even if we hoarded gold for several years, we would not be able to afford such a treasure!'

The prince sighed in exasperation. The whole palace was talking about this extraordinary *bunga mas*—a bouquet of flowers crafted with branches and leaves of silver and flowers of pure gold. The *bunga mas* was a normal tributary gift from one kingdom to another but this one was extraordinary because of the fact that its twelve exquisite lotus blossoms were life size and encrusted with tiny white and pink pearls. But the prince was unimpressed. He snapped, 'Are we selling ourselves and Langkasuka for a mere *bunga mas*?'

His mother replied in a placating voice, 'Please have some forbearance, Perita. The *bunga mas* is an offering of friendship, for which we should be grateful. You know that your father and I do not covet such treasures; if the need arises, we will willingly sell the *bunga mas* to the wealthy Tang merchants to pay for food and other necessities to meet the needs of the kingdom.'

Raja Perita was silent. He knew that his mother was telling him the truth if not in its *entirety*. He knew that his parents, his father in particular, led simple lives. Their jewels and the palace adornments were ancestral heirlooms and they only replaced clothes once a year just before the Spring water festival. The queen drew in a deep breath and continued, 'Chula, Satra and Yala will be coming to keep you company. You know that you have a lot to talk about and Maharaja Lela has selected the best court dancers to entertain our honoured guests!'

The prince tossed his head and retorted, 'Mother, I've seen "Manohra" performed hundreds of times!' and stormed out.

The prince did not notice the handmaiden but she looked at him through her lowered lashes. She had heard all the rumours about him . . . strange stories that he was possessed by a dark spirit; that he roamed the palace at night, weeping and talking to himself; that prisoners were disappearing . . . She was not prepared for the reality of seeing Raja Perita in the flesh. The skin like ivory, the unnaturally bright eyes fringed by dark lashes. He took her breath away and she thought that he must surely be one of the *orang bunyan*, the faerie.

Since the incident in the forest, the prince avoided the sun as much as he could; his glorious tan faded and his skin grew as pale as that of his mother. His dark smouldering eyes contrasted sharply with his pale cheeks; but he was never quite himself again. Whereas he had been cheerfully hedonistic and wilful before, now he was cold and withdrawn, with an aura of dark energy. The prince continued with practising the *sundang* and *lembing*, spears used for hunting but only in the shade or after sundown.

That evening after she had been dismissed, Rawan ran silently down the steps; she was barefooted like everyone else as it was a sign of extreme disrespect to wear sandals or shoes in the palace. She ran across the corridor to the opposite side of the palace where the king had his audience hall. Holding her breath, she tiptoed until she had reached the small side entrance to the hall. The handmaiden heard the sound of music and laughter coming from within and slipped in unnoticed. She hid behind the high latticed wooden screens which were placed at intervals around the hall. The lattice allowed her to spy on what was going on without being seen by anyone. The hall was lit by numerous candles and torches placed along the walls. The king and queen sat on a raised platform; the Sri Vijayan prince sat to their right, with his retinue seated behind him, while Raja Perita sat on their left. His friends were seated near him. The rest of the court was seated behind the king and queen.

Rawan watched awestruck as elaborately costumed dancers performed the slow, intricate, graceful court dance known as Manohra. They were accompanied by musicians playing on traditional instruments. When the dance was over, the court was surprised when three young musicians came on stage and started playing a fast-paced rhythmic song while a beautiful dancer in a gold embroidered chemise and long flowing skirt came on stage and performed a graceful yet fast dance. The tip of her fingers and the palm of her hand were decorated with red henna—they traced out intricate patterns of delicate vines, leaves and flowers all the way up to her forearm. Even her forehead and temple were decorated with henna.

The prince and his friends were enraptured by the music and the dance; they had never seen anyone dance like this before and guessed that the Sri Vijayan prince had brought them with him from Palembang. The dancer displayed extraordinary skill and stamina while executing the dance, barely breaking a sweat. Raja Perita sensed that her heart beat was only slightly elevated, something only a warrior in peak form would have been able to achieve.

When the dance was over, the beautiful dancer picked up a handful of jasmine flowers and threw them in the direction of Raja Perita. A shower of flowers fell around him and he caught a fragrant blossom in his fingers before it could land on his lap. The prince kissed it and placed it in the silk pouch hidden under his tunic. The dancer and the musicians bowed gracefully with palms together to show their gratitude. Then the four of them picked up their things to leave.

The handmaiden caught her breath and felt her heart contract in despair when she saw the prince kissing the flower. She quickly retreated into the shadows so that no one would see her. The king and queen, followed by the rest of the court soon returned to their quarters in the palace or home in Kota Aur. The Sri Vijayan Prince and his retinue walked out of the palace to take a leisurely walk to their ship, which was moored in the harbour.

Prince Perita and his friends decided to remain in the hall. Satra said, 'That dancer from Sri Vijaya was something else. Quite a beauty and did you notice how quickly she moved? Her feet were almost flying . . . It was exhilarating!'

Yala retorted, 'That's because you are so used to the slow dance of the Manohra!'

'I quite like the Manohra, myself. It's graceful and courtly, with very deliberate movements . . .' mused Chula.

Yala snorted, 'You and your courtly ways, Chula! I've seen you eyeing the Queen's new handmaiden . . . Nong . . . what's her name?'

Chula countered, 'Me eyeing a maiden? Yala, I admire lovely maidens from afar as I would the precious lotus blossom. You on the other hand . . . why I've seen you almost breathing down the neck of . . .'

The prince looked up at Chula and cut in, 'She's fetching all right, but a bit of a snoop . . . she probably knows more about what goes on in court than Maharaja Lela himself . . .'

Then he turned his head and gave a sharp look at the latticed window. The handmaiden started with fright and silently ran to her chamber as quickly as she could. He looked at Yala and added, 'And her name is Rawan, by the way.'

His friends looked at him expectantly but Raja Perita continued in a more reflective voice, 'Actually, I agree with Satra; there was something about the beauty from Sri Vijaya . . . something quite extraordinary. I've never encountered anyone so alive before . . .'

The three friends looked at one another quizzically, not quite sure what the prince meant. Chula decided to change the subject and asked the prince, 'Rumour has it that the visit from the prince of Sri Vijaya is more than just for pleasure . . . is it true?'

Raja Perita said ruefully, 'I'm afraid it's true. Apparently, the ancient kingdom of Langkasuka is now a vassal of that new upstart Empire of Sri Vijaya. They owe us now—body and soul. In fact, I may have to marry the sister of the condescending Rajaputra Chandra Kinnara.'

Yala burst out laughing. He said, 'Kinnara? How romantic! Aren't Kinnaras devoted lovers who are half-man and half-bird?'

Chula said primly, 'Half-swan actually, but Rajaputra Chandra doesn't have any wings or feathers as we all saw. I don't know if we should congratulate you or commiserate with you, my lord, Perita. But if his sister is as good looking as he is, this marriage might not be such a burden after all . . .'

Yala said with a mischievous smile, 'Can you imagine a pretty little princess ordering our arrogant prince around?'

Raja Perita frowned at him but before he could say anything, Satra interjected, 'The Rajaputeri of Sri Vijaya can order me around anytime!'

Everyone burst out laughing. There was a pause before Yala asked unexpectedly, 'What about the rumours of a rising power to the north . . . threatening even Sri Vijaya itself?'

This time it was Chula who replied, 'It's true what they say, that the walls really have ears! We are not supposed to know this, but it seems that Langkasuka is the proverbial mouse-deer caught between two mighty elephants—Sri Vijaya to the South and the Khmer Kingdom to the north. When Raja Jayavarman returned to Chenla decades ago . . .'

Satra interrupted him, 'Who is Raja Jayavarman?'

Chula said patronizingly, 'Allow me to explain, Satra . . . Jayavarman was the former king of Chenla. Anyway, he succeeded in uniting Chenla with Funan, to create a single Khmer Kingdom. Rumour has it that he managed to get hold of a priest all the way from Bharat to perform a secret ritual on top of a mountain so that he could declare himself, *Chakravartin* . . . which means Ruler of the World, by the way. The ritual was supposed to give him some form of magical power . . . and he ruled the Khmers for over sixty years! Luckily for Langkasuka, he was content to leave us alone. We have just learnt that the *Chakravartin* has been dead for some time and that his grandson, known as Indravarman is eyeing Langkasuka . . .'

Everyone looked at Chula with a mixture of astonishment and admiration. This time it was Yala who asked the question, 'And how do you know all this?'

Chula continued, 'I know all this because I sometimes get to sit in meetings between the King and some of the important foreign visitors . . .'

Raja Perita commented thoughtfully, 'I guess that explains my mother's anxiousness to form an alliance with Sri Vijaya.'

Satra said, 'The choice is obvious, at least to me. On the one hand we have a powerful land empire intent on making us their vassal while on the other hand we have a powerful sea empire also intent on making us their vassal . . . but with a princess and a jewelled tree thrown in . . .'

Yala frowned and interrupted him, 'Why don't we fight for our kingdom? Why is it necessary to form an alliance with one or the other?' Satra and Chula were surprised to see that he appeared to be genuinely upset.

Chula rubbed his chin before replying. After a pause, he said, 'Hmmm . . . I think it's because we are too . . . umm . . . peaceable. Our king believes in following the way of nonviolence and the kingdom has devoted its wealth and resources in building temples and offering its hospitality to learned scholars, priests, poets and dancers from all over the world. They are our true treasures . . .'

Raja Perita said briskly, 'Everyone knows that the king, my father, has devoted his life to following the Middle Path according to the teachings of the Enlightened One. Going to war is not acceptable to him.'

'But what happens if Langkasuka is attacked by another kingdom? Although we have a small army, it's not nearly enough . . .' muttered Yala darkly.

Not wanting to offend the prince, Chula turned towards Raja Perita and asked, 'What is your opinion about this, my lord?'

But Raja Perita was not paying attention to them any more. He said almost to himself, 'I wonder . . .' Then he got up and told his friends, 'I need some air now but and I'll be back soon!'

Leaving them to chat, he walked swiftly out of the hall and through another side door, out of the palace. He scanned the garden and quickly picked up the scent he was searching for. The prince moved with what seemed extraordinary velocity, an ability he developed after his attack. But in effect time was slowing down for him—while he moved everything around him came to a virtual standstill. Raja Perita quickly caught up with the group he was tracking—it was the Prince of Sri Vijaya and his party.

When he drew close to them, he concealed his presence by hiding behind the shadow of a large tree. He leapt up silently on to the largest branch and landed cat-like on his feet. It created a slight movement, which made the prince and the palace guards look around but they failed to see anything amiss. It was close enough for him to hear what they were saying without anyone being aware of his presence. He heard Raja Chandra address the dancer, 'Has the Prince of Langkasuka made a favourable impression on you, dear sister?'

The dancer replied animatedly, 'I'm quite spellbound by his charms. They say that his mother has faerie blood, perhaps that's why he looks so . . . alive! His eyes are like glowing ambers deep in the fire . . .' She stopped herself and then continued in a hesitant voice, 'But they also say that he is possessed by a dark spirit and that he is not really human . . .'

Raja Chandra laughed, 'I'm sure Raja Perita is as human as the rest of us! But you sound as if you have already fallen for this prince with the bright eyes . . .'

The dancer turned towards him and asked hesitantly, 'Chandra, do you think he . . . likes me . . . a little?'

Raja Chandra reassured her, 'My beautiful sister Chaiya, how could he not love you? Your fire burns as bright as his . . . and you saw the way he looked at you as you danced . . .'

Their voices were fading away as they were walking towards the harbour. Raja Perita leapt down from the branch of the tree and landed as silently and as gracefully as a cat, crouching low on the ground. He stood up and hesitated, before finally deciding to follow the brother and sister. He was careful to conceal himself, moving swiftly from the shadow of one tree to another. When they reached the water's edge, Chaiya and Chandra were helped unto a large *sampan*. They sat on cushioned seats while six men rowed them towards their *perahu*, a giant five-masted ship swaying to and fro in the gentle waves. Chaiya turned to look back at the shore and was visibly startled to see the prince standing on the beach, gazing at her intently. She gasped and her brother turned to look as well, but the prince was no longer there.

Chandra asked, 'What is it? Why do you look so shocked?'

Chaiya replied, 'It was him! The Prince of Langkasuka . . .'

'Are you sure? He couldn't have followed us . . . he was still in the palace when we left.'

'You're right, Brother. It was probably just a sailor standing on the beach.'

'But I didn't see anyone, Chaiya,' replied Chandra.

Raja Perita could not cross the water and he did not want to be seen by anyone. He had moved swiftly into the shadow of the nearest tree, faster than the eye could see and made his way back to the grand hall of the palace. He was in such a hurry, he did not notice a pair of eyes spying on him as he entered the hall to continue the banter with his friends.

* * *

Rawan went out of her way to attract his attention. She even went to the kitchen to carry his favourite dish up to his chamber for him . . .

But the cook was suspicious. She snapped at her, 'Nong Rawan, why are you here? You are the queen's own handmaiden, it is your duty to serve her only!'

Rawan protested, 'The queen does not need me in attendance all the time! Why shouldn't I serve the prince as well?'

The cook looked at her in the eye and said sternly, 'Rawan, do not get carried away by your foolish ideas . . . I know that almost every man in court is captivated by your looks but he is a royal prince . . . far above your station. Do not attempt to entice the prince!'

The handmaiden tossed her beautiful head and said in a defiant voice, 'Why? It is not unheard of for a handmaiden to marry royalty! Why should I listen to a mere cook?'

The cook actually turned pale and gasped, 'Are you insane, child? You have no idea what is going on . . . what he is . . . For your own sake, stay away from him!'

'Stay away from whom?' a voice interjected. It was Raja Perita's servant, come to fetch his food.

Rawan looked startled but the cook replied quickly, 'No one that concerns you, Bujang! Here, the prince's food is ready!' and handed him the silver tray loaded with food. Bujang walked away with the tray of food while Rawan looked at his retreating figure dejectedly.

Rawan's attraction to the prince had grown into an obsession and the cook's warnings fell on deaf ears. She contrived to be present whenever the prince went to talk with his mother but Raja Perita seemed oblivious to her presence. Finally she sneaked into his quarters while he was away one evening. She frantically checked his pillows and bed sheets and went through his belongings before she found what she was looking for—a few strands of his long hair caught in his ivory comb. With bated breath, she carefully pulled them out with her fingers and placed them in a little cloth pouch . . .

Rawan almost jumped out of her skin when a voice said, 'Rawan! What are you doing here?'

She spun around, her face pale with fear and was relieved to see that it was Bujang. But his face was pale and drawn and he looked furious. Before she could think of anything to say, Bujang snapped at her, 'Don't you know that no one is allowed into the prince's chambers without permission?'

Rawan said apologetically, 'The queen asked me to check Raja Perita's quarters . . . sometimes the maid forgets to clean his room . . . properly.'

He told her sharply, 'You better return to the servants' quarters before the prince returns! I'm already in enough trouble as it is!'

The handmaiden bowed her head in contrition and said, 'I'm sorry, Bujang. I never meant to cause you any harm!'

He said with a smile, 'It's all right, Rawan. After all we were childhood friends. We need to help one another . . .'

Rawan flashed him a brilliant smile and said, 'We will always be friends, Bujang!' Although she was genuinely sorry about deceiving Bujang, she could not stop from smiling to herself as she got up and ran out of the chamber.

Her next step was to see Tok Dukun. She found out where he lived from her sister, who still sometimes came to the palace to lend Rawan a hand. Rawan asked her casually one day, 'Elder sister, where does Tok Dukun live? I heard that many of the court ladies see him for health problems . . .'

Her sister said in alarm, 'Why do you need to see Tok Dukun? Are you unwell, Rawan?'

Rawan said with a shrug, 'It's nothing serious, really. It's just that lately I'm having difficulty sleeping and my appetite is poor.'

She had no trouble convincing her sister as it was quite true that she was looking somewhat pale and thin compared to her usual vivacious self. Once she had the necessary information, she took leave from the queen to pay him a visit. When she arrived unannounced, Tok Dukun was surprised to see her. Although the handmaidens and ladies of the court frequently came to see him for all manner of potions, they were mostly older women. Sometimes it was for genuine health reasons but more often they were interested in beauty potions . . .

Rawan diffidently climbed up the steps to his modest wooden cottage. She seated herself on a woven mat on the floor and he offered her the customary betel quid, which she politely declined. She said hesitantly, 'Tok, there is a young man at court . . . I have fallen in love with . . . I cannot live without him but he ignores me completely. Is there a potion to help me win his love?'

Tok Dukun was even more surprised by her confession. He found it hard to believe that this ravishing young beauty had difficulty in beguiling any young man . . . He said gently, 'Nong Rawan, I make healing herbs and potions to treat people who are unwell; occasionally even beauty potions . . . A love potion is another animal altogether! We all know that love is something which must be freely given and earned . . . Is it wise for you to pursue this matter further?'

Rawan shed tears of desperation from her beautiful dark eyes. She said in between sobs, 'What am I to do, Tok? I cannot even eat or sleep without thinking of him; day and night . . . If you cannot help me, I don't think I can go on living . . .'

The kindly old man was genuinely alarmed. He said as convincingly as he could, 'Do not lose hope, child. There are many worthy young men out there. In a few months' time, you will be wondering what you ever saw in this person to begin with!'

She replied sadly, 'How can I go on living if I have no rest or respite from this fever?'

Seeing her looking so crestfallen, Tok Dukun felt sorry for her. He sighed and said, 'Nong Rawan, I do this against my better judgement . . . I will make the potion which will bind a person's affection . . . at least for a short while. Perhaps he will fall in love with you of his own accord . . .'

The young maiden brightened visibly upon hearing his words. She fumbled through her belt and took out the pouch. She continued earnestly, 'I've even brought a few strands of his hair . . . I've heard that you need the hair of a person to make a love potion . . .'

The old man sighed and said, 'Let me have the strands of his hair . . .'

Rawan handed over the few strands of hair to Tok Dukun. She watched with bated breath as he burnt the strands of hair in a tiny clay container while whispering an incantation over them. As he uttered the spell in a singsong voice, the mixture in the pot glowed with a faint light. Then he poured some water into the container together with a few drops of tamarind juice and a mixture of shredded herbs, and carefully stirred the mixture with a wooden stick while whispering another incantation. The mixture in the pot glowed and bubbled by itself. Finally, he handed the clay pot to Rawan, 'Please drink the mixture and make sure you drink every drop!'

The potion was bitter, with a tinge of sourness from the tamarind but Rawan lost no time in drinking the concoction. Tok Dukun then asked her for a few strands of her own hair. She plucked out a few strands of her hair and handed them to him. Tok Dukun took the hair and placed them in another clay container. He performed the same ritual as before, but this time he added a few drops of perfume and coconut oil into the ashes. After carefully blending the concoction, he poured the liquid into a tiny clay pot and handed it to her. He said, 'Place a few drops of this perfume behind each ear and place this container underneath his pillow before he goes to bed tonight!'

That night, she applied the potion behind each of her ears and waited for him in the shadows of the corridor. She knew that he always passed that way when he returned late from a night out with his friends. He was surprised to see her and enquired, 'Are you not the queen's handmaiden? Why are you not in your chambers so late at night?'

She lied, 'My lord, the queen was worried about you and asked me to keep an eye on you . . . you have not been well lately . . .'

His voice was sardonic, when he replied, 'Are you talking about my mother or about yourself? My mother would have instructed a guard to keep an eye on me . . . not her handmaiden. I am not entirely blind, you know!'

She blushed and lowered her long lashes and admitted, 'My lord, can you blame a poor maiden for worrying about you?'

He sensed her modesty was contrived but she was so beautiful . . . He was drawn towards her and stretched out her hand to touch her. He said, 'I remember my mother calling you, Rawan . . . a lovely name . . .'

He could hear her heart beating and sensed the warm blood flowing underneath her skin . . . She was so alive and warm . . . Then Raja Perita froze. A faint fragrance was in the air, the scent of champaka and the memory of the night he was attacked flashed in his mind. Horror overwhelmed him; what was he thinking of? Was he turning into that hateful demon?

Rawan gasped, 'What's the matter, my lord? You look unwell . . .'

He pushed her away and cried out, 'Go . . . go away! Stay away from me! Don't ever approach me again!'

Then he turned and fled to his chamber, leaving the handmaiden looking shocked and humiliated.

Maharaja Lela Seeks the Truth

The next morning, the calm of a new day was shattered by the scream of a maid. She had almost fallen over a dead body in the palace courtyard, unnoticed in the pale light of dawn. Nong Rawan, the queen's beautiful handmaiden was dead. She was lying on the floor with her long hair spread out behind her. There were traces of blood on her neck and her face was completely pale, as if all her blood had been drained from her body.

Maharaja Lela was summoned to the scene; he examined the wound on her neck carefully to see if it was inflicted with a weapon. The chamberlain also checked her hands and her nails to see if she had put up a fight, he nodded when he saw faint traces of blood on the tip of her nails. His eyes caught something glinting in the folds of the long silk scarf she tied around her waist like all the other handmaidens. He carefully fished the object out—it was a gold arm bracelet in the shape of a fern leaf. After making sure that he was not being observed, he slipped it into his coin pouch.

He summoned the maid and asked her, 'Did you move or touch Nong Rawan's body when you found her this morning?'

The maid shook her head and replied fervently, 'No my lord! I was too scared to touch her. It's bad luck to touch someone who has been murdered!'

He asked the maid a few other questions but she obviously knew nothing.

The next person the chamberlain talked to was the cook. She was always up by dawn to prepare the morning meal. He said, 'I'm sure by now you must have heard that Rawan has passed away . . . and that her death is not natural.'

The cook looked distressed, 'Yes, my lord, Maharaja Lela. Poor Rawan . . . so young and beautiful. But I did warn her . . .'

Maharaja Lela quickly asked, 'What exactly did you warn her about, Cook?'

The cook looked abashed. Finally she replied, 'Forgive me, my lord, but I thought she had feelings for the prince. I told her that he was above her station and she should not attempt to entice him . . .'

Maharaja Lela nodded, 'You were right to advise her . . . such matters usually do not end well. So the queen's handmaiden was in love with the prince . . . Do you happen to know if the prince returned her love?'

The cook looked surprised by his question. She frowned and said, 'I really can't say, my lord. As far as I know, he did not seem to be especially interested . . . but one can never really know the truth about these things . . .'

Maharaja Lela changed the subject, 'The other matter I wanted to bring up is the prince's food. Has there been any changes in his need for . . . blood?'

The cook looked surprised, 'No, my lord. I prepare a small bowl of rice accompanied by a large bowl of *gulai bayam* every day, for the prince's afternoon meal . . .' She lowered her voice and added, 'A cup of blood is added to the broth, before being served; as far as I know that is all the prince eats.'

Maharaja Lela nodded and said, 'Apart from the queen, we are perhaps the only ones in the palace who know about his need for blood. Are you sure that none of the other kitchen staff know about this?'

The cook looked offended and said, 'My lord! I'm the only one allowed to cook his meals and I always make sure I'm not being watched!' She was careful not to mention that Satra had already guessed about the secret ingredient in the *gulai bayam* some time ago.

While the chamberlain was talking to the cook, another handmaiden quickly went to the queen's chamber to tell her what had happened. The queen, who had just awakened looked shocked and pale when she heard the news. The chambermaid helped her to dress and the cook brought in her breakfast but the queen was too distraught to eat. She walked as quickly as she could to her small audience room on the ground floor and asked to see Maharaja Lela.

Before long, Maharaja Lela was seated in front of her. The queen said in a worried voice, 'I never imagined something like this could happen, Maharaja Lela! Poor

Rawan . . . I'm terrified to even think who could be behind this horrible crime . . .'

Maharaja Lela replied, his voice impassive as always, 'I have questioned the palace servants who normally spend the night at the palace, my lady. But no one seems to know anything about this tragic event.' He cleared his throat and added quietly, 'My lady, I need to inform you that the wound inflicted on Rawan is very similar to the wound suffered by the prince that fateful night . . . and the other thing I need to disclose is that I found the prince's bracelet in the possession of the maid.'

The queen turned pale upon hearing his words. After a long pause, she said, 'What does this mean? Is it possible that the prince gave her the bracelet?'

Maharaja Lela looked thoughtful. He said, 'That is one possible explanation, however, it implies that the prince had feelings for her . . . It's also possible that she took the item herself . . . without his knowledge.'

'Yes, I see,' the queen replied. Then she asked him hesitantly, 'You will of course keep the information about the bracelet to yourself. Could you also please ask the prince, discretely of course, if he has any knowledge of this . . . horrible event. We both know about his strange illness. Perhaps he may be willing to confide in you . . . certain things he would not be willing to tell his mother . . .'

The royal chamberlain said, 'Of course, my lady. You can count on my discretion in all matters. I will speak to the prince myself, the moment after he wakes up. Have no fear about this; I hear and obey your every command.'

The next person Maharaja Lela talked to was Raja Perita's man servant, Bujang. He was relieved to find out from Bujang that the prince was still asleep. Bujang said, 'To attempt to awaken my lord prince before noon is to wager with one's life.'

Maharaja Lela raised his eyebrows and said, 'Why would you say that, Bujang?'

Bujang replied, 'My lord is not like himself if he is awakened too early . . . his eyes become bloodshot and he goes into a rage at the slightest provocation . . . forgive me, I should not disparage my master.'

The chamberlain assured him, 'I value your honesty, Bujang. Nothing you say to me will be repeated. Now tell me, do you know anything about Rawan's sudden death?'

Tears sprang into Bujang's eyes. His voice shook when he said, 'She should not have died in that horrible way . . .'

'So you knew her?' Maharaja Lela asked.

'Yes, we grew up together in the same village. Her sister was also a handmaiden and Rawan was really happy to get the post as the queen's handmaiden . . . it was a dream come true for her . . .' his voice trailed away and he had to wipe away the tears which sprang in his eyes again.

Maharaja Lela nodded, he already knew as much. He tried to sound as sympathetic as he could, 'I'm deeply sorry for your loss, Bujang. But I've heard from one of the palace servants that she had fallen for the prince. Did you notice anything to indicate that this could be true?'

Bujang's face darkened and he cast his eyes down. Then he took in a deep breath, lifted his head and said, 'I'm sorry to say that it was true. Once I even caught her lurking in the corridor here, waiting for the prince. I warned her not to do that again . . . the queen frowns upon such behaviour on the part of her handmaidens.'

Maharaja Lela, 'Young women can be impetuous at times . . . But I also get the feeling that you were perhaps in love with Rawan?'

Tears sprang to the young's man eyes once again. For a moment he could not speak. Then he said, 'It's true that I loved her, my lord . . . but she thought I was not good enough for her . . . she only had eyes for the prince . . .'

Maharaja nodded and said, 'One last question; do you happen to know if anyone else in the palace had feelings for the queen's handmaiden?'

Bujang looked perplexed. He finally said, 'She sometimes mentioned that she had a "secret admirer" but she never revealed his name to me . . .'

When the interrogation was over, Maharaja Lela instructed Bujang not to tell the prince anything that had transpired that morning. Raja Perita did not wake up until late afternoon as always. Maharaja Lela did not confront him until after he had dressed and had his mid-day meal.

The prince appeared truly shocked to hear of the handmaiden's death from the chamberlain. He appeared to have no knowledge of Rawan's death. Undeterred, Maharaja Lela continued, 'Some of the palace servants have said that the queen's handmaiden was in fact in love with you, perhaps you also had feelings for her, my lord?'

Raja Perita was annoyed. He replied in a cold voice, 'You have the audacity to confront me with such a question, Maharaja Lela! No, I did not have any feelings for her . . .

although I did of course notice her beauty; as I'm sure everyone in the palace did!'

The chamberlain was not to be put off so easily. He continued in a polite but firm voice, 'Your humble slave means no disrespect, my lord. There is no question that you have the right to bestow your attention on whomever you please. But did you by any chance give her a gift? Even a jewel, perhaps?'

The prince looked surprised at his question. He said, 'No, my lord, Maharaja Lela, I did not give Rawan any gifts. And if I had given her jewels, I don't remember it at all!'

Maharaja Lela cleared his throat and pressed on with his questions, 'I have information my lord, that you came home late last night; perhaps you had a word with her?'

Raja Perita's pale cheeks flushed and he took in a deep breath. Finally he said, 'Yes, I spoke with her last night. In fact, she was waiting for me, I think. But I told her to . . . to go away. To think that I might have been the last person to . . .' He frowned and stopped himself from completing the sentence.

Maharaja Lela was about to ask another question but the prince looked him defiantly in the eye and said, 'Enough! I feel bad enough for behaving like a coward . . . I refuse to answer any more of your questions! Now leave us!'

Before the chamberlain left the room, the prince shot back at him, 'In case you have any doubts, the queen's handmaiden was very much alive when I left her, last night!'

Maharaja Lela wasted no time to report to the queen. He told her, 'The prince appeared to be genuinely shocked by the news of your handmaiden's death; I have no doubt that he did not commit this heinous deed . . . or at least he has no knowledge of it . . .'

The queen appeared relieved and perplexed at the same time. She asked him, 'But what does it all mean, Maharaja Lela?'

The chamberlain said gravely, 'It means that either there is a malevolent supernatural agent at work at Kota Aur or someone masquerading as one, my lady.' He paused and added, 'I also believe that my lord prince knows something about this dark entity but he does not want to divulge any information . . . and I suspect that his young servant, Bujang, is also hiding a secret . . . '

The queen said, 'I fear that the prince may be in danger . . . as he was the last person to see Rawan alive. Please inform the *hulubalang* not to let him out of the palace until the mystery is solved.'

The next morning, Maharaja Lela had a talk with the prince's three friends in his own audience room. Unlike the queen's opulent audience room, it was sparsely furnished with mats on the floor and decorated with shields and spears on the walls. He had summoned them to the palace that morning but could not meet them because of the audience with the queen.

Maharaja Lela spoke sternly, 'You all know that a terrible tragedy has struck the palace. As all three of you were with the prince last night, I need to know if you were aware of anything amiss.'

Chula answered, 'My lord, Maharaja Lela, as far as I know there was nothing out of the ordinary yesterday. We had tea at the Green Jade Teahouse where we were entertained by dancers. We left the teahouse before it closed and escorted the prince to the palace. Then we all went to our respective houses . . .'

'So none of you followed him to the palace itself?' asked Maharaja Lela.

This time Satra answered, 'No my lord, none of us followed the prince to the palace . . . we left him at the palace gate, as always. My lord prince is stronger and faster than any of us and does not need our protection!'

Maharaja Lela replied dryly, 'I was not implying that he needed protection, Lord Satra . . . I just wanted to know if any of you had witnessed his encounter with the handmaiden . . .'

All three young men were silent. Then Maharaja Lela said, 'I am about to disclose something to you . . . a secret which must never leave these four walls.'

The three young men sat up and looked at him attentively. Maharaja Lela paused to weigh his words and said gravely, 'That night, after being attacked at the temple, Raja Perita was at death's door, and no treatment or potion seemed able to heal him. Fortunately, some months ago, we discovered that human blood could cure the prince. The prince has blood added to his food everyday . . .'

All three of them lowered their head and the royal chamberlain could have sworn that Yala was trying to conceal his laughter. Maharaja Lela said sharply, 'Lord Yala! Did you find what I just said amusing?'

Yala raised his head and said, 'Forgive me, my lord, Maharaja Lela! We have known about this for quite some time now . . .'

Satra added, 'My lord, the prince himself told us about his need for blood!'

It was Maharaja Lela's turn to look baffled. He did not like being taken by surprise as he always prided himself in knowing everything that was going on in the palace.

Chula explained, 'My lord, the prince gradually became aware that blood was being added to his food . . . although everyone tried to keep it a secret, even from him. But it is not possible to conceal something like this from a person who can smell a civet hiding among the bushes from fifty paces . . .'

Maharaja Lela sighed and said, 'Thank you, my lord, Chula. I should have realized that a secret like this could not be kept for long . . . I disclosed this information to you to find out if any of you had witnessed anything strange about the prince's behaviour . . .'

Yala said, 'If you are asking if we have ever seen the prince biting anyone in the neck . . . than the answer is, no! Raja Perita is his usual arrogant disdainful self!'

Before he dismissed them, Maharaja Lela told them, 'Raja Perita has been forbidden to leave the palace until this matter is resolved. I request that each of you take turns to keep the prince company to make sure that he does not stray away from the palace grounds. And I warn all of you again that this information must never leave these four walls!'

Chula assured him, 'Have no fear, Father. We have all made a covenant not to reveal the prince's secret to anyone!'

Maharaja Lela pondered over the information he had gathered so far. He felt that he may have missed a clue. But it was the cook who alerted him that something was wrong—Bujang had not come to the kitchen to pick up the prince's dinner that evening. Maharaja Lela immediately asked to see Raja Perita's servant, Bujang. One of the guards told him, 'My lord, Maharaja Lela; Bujang has not turned up to carry out his duties this evening and the prince is still asleep in his chamber.'

The usually impassive chamberlain actually looked alarmed and said, 'Quickly, follow me! We have to check on the prince.'

He rushed into the prince's chamber, accompanied by two of his personal guards. The prince was in deep slumber and the remains of his mid-day meal were still on the low wooden table by his bedside. The chamberlain touched the prince's pale face and his face grew grave—it was deathly cold. But when he looked at his face more closely, the chamberlain was relieved to find out that the prince was still breathing. He turned to the food on the table, particularly the remains of the *gulai bayam* and held it up to his nose. He could not detect anything amiss. Then he noticed something new on the table—rich and dark in colour, it appeared to be a dessert made of sticky *pulut* rice, palm sugar and coconut milk. The chamberlain sniffed and tasted it; it was sweet, perhaps a little too sweet. There was an aftertaste too, which seemed familiar . . .

Finally he drew in a deep breath and said, '*Kekubung* . . . the prince has been poisoned with *kekubung*. The crushed seeds are added to a strongly flavoured drink or food to conceal the taste. Fortunately, it is rarely fatal and merely renders the victim insensible.'

He propped the prince up on his pillow and gently shook him. Raja Perita gasped for breath and opened his eyes. He then closed them again, turning his head away with a groan. Maharaja Lela instructed the guard, 'We need to revive the prince . . . one of you summon Tok Dukun while the other please bring up the prince's dinner from the kitchen . . . and don't forget to inform the queen.'

When the queen arrived, Maharaja Lela quickly told her about his suspicions. He picked up the silver bowl containing the dessert and walked to the kitchen himself. Cook was still there looking harassed and wringing her hands in consternation; she had already heard that the prince had been poisoned. Maharaja Lela's presence in her kitchen alarmed her even more. He said, 'Calm down Cook, no one is blaming you. I just wanted to ask you if you made this dessert for the prince?'

Cook said, 'Yes, my lord. I made the same dessert for the entire royal household today . . . why, is something wrong?'

Maharaja Lela handed her the poisoned bowl and said, 'Do you notice anything odd or different about this bowl of sweet *pulut*?'

The cook sniffed and tasted the sticky rice pudding the way he had done. She said, 'It is darker and much sweeter than the dessert I made . . . I use palm sugar sparingly as the king is practising austerity . . . and there is an odd aftertaste. I think someone must have added extra palm sugar in the dessert.'

Maharaja Lela nodded and said, 'Just as I thought . . . and you are sure no one could have tampered with the prince's food?'

The cook looked upset, 'My lord, you know that I prepare and plate all his food myself. No one is even allowed near his food. I handed the tray to Bujang himself, before he carried it to the prince's chambers.'

Maharaja Lela thanked her, much to the cook's surprise before returning to check on the prince again. Once Raja Perita had been awakened from his sleep, Maharaja Lela returned to his quarters in a sombre mood. He had a foreboding that tragedy was about to strike again.

The next morning the palace was in uproar, the gardener had found Bujang's body near the small stream which ran in the garden. He had cuts on his arms and he was clutching a blood-stained *keris* in his lifeless hand. Maharaja Lela examined the cuts on his arms but he knew these were not what killed him. He examined Bujang's neck and found the same deep wounds as that on Rawan's neck. Bujang's body was removed from the garden and carried to his home in Kota Aur.

The queen did not ask to see the chamberlain until almost midday. She looked even more drawn than before; her face was pale and there were dark shadows beneath her eyes. She said, 'I dare not even ask you about the terrible tragedy that has befallen us, my lord . . . first my handmaiden and now Raja Perita's servant . . . I had to ask

Satra to take over Bujang's duties as the prince does not trust anyone else now.'

'If it makes you feel any better, my lady, I am more convinced than ever that the prince had nothing to do with it . . .' replied Maharaja Lela.

The queen looked up sharply, and said, 'How would you know that, my lord?'

Maharaja Lela said, 'Bujang mentioned that he had caught Nong Rawan hiding in the corridors to catch a glimpse of the prince . . .' He paused when he saw the surprised look on the queen's face and continued apologetically, 'It seems she was quite a flirt . . . in any case it made me realize that he could have been spying on her on the night she was killed . . . in which case he could have caught a glimpse of the murderer . . .'

'And you know that it was not the prince because . . .?' the queen asked with bated breath.

'Bujang also suspected that she had a secret admirer or lover whose identity he took with him to his grave, unfortunately for everyone,' Maharaja Lela said even more apologetically. 'Of course, it could have been the prince, my lady, but I think not. Bujang had wounds on his arms which meant that he confronted the killer in an attempt to avenge Rawan. Bujang drugged the prince to keep him out of the way. I believe if he thought the prince was the killer, he could have . . . ahem . . . given him a lethal poison. While *kekubung* is known to render a person unconscious, it is rarely fatal.'

The queen drew in a deep breath and said gratefully, 'Thank you for clearing my doubts about my son, my lord!

But we are still facing the same dilemma . . . we cannot clear my son's name until the real killer is caught.'

'And we have to face the possibility that the killer might strike again . . .' added the royal chamberlain gravely.

The Moon Garden

The queen was so perturbed by the two horrific deaths which shattered the calm of the palace in the space of a week that she decided to summon Tok Dukun. This time, she asked Maharaja Lela to be present as well. The queen asked Tok Dukun, 'The last time we met, Tok Dukun, you mentioned that a creature called a *pontianak* could have attacked the prince. Is it possible that there is such a creature in our kingdom, preying on people?'

Tok Dukun replied, 'I am at a loss, my lady.' He paused and added, 'When I first treated the prince, that seemed the most likely explanation. But now, I don't think so. I don't think Nong Rawan and Bujang were attacked by a *pontianak*; something more sinister is at work . . . and I'm afraid it is beyond my ken.'

The queen looked pale and drawn. She said, 'We need to get to the bottom of this, Tok Dukun. I simply fail to understand what is going on! Why would anyone want to take their lives?'

Tok Dukun cleared his throat and said, 'Please forgive your humble servant, but there is perhaps something I should mention. Nong Rawan came to visit me a few days before her death. She wanted me to make a potion for her . . . a love potion.'

Both the queen and Maharaja Lela looked surprised and exchanged glances. Before the queen could say anything, Maharaja Lela asked him, 'Did she give you the name of the person the potion was intended for?'

Tok Dukun replied apologetically, 'No, I'm afraid not. She gave me a few strands of his hair. I just assumed they belonged to one of the young lords.'

The queen asked, 'Is there anyone else we could turn to for assistance, Tok Dukun? I suppose many people come to see you for potions and you must hear some news and stories.'

Tok Dukun thought for a while before replying, 'My lady, there is a small temple on the outskirts of Kota Aur. I heard that the priest who resides there is from the ancient land of Bharat and people claim that he possesses knowledge of the ancients. He may be able to offer some insight into the matter.'

Maharaja Lela interposed, 'With your permission, my lady, I will visit this temple with Tok Dukun tomorrow.'

When Tok Dukun had left the palace, the queen asked, 'How is my dear husband, the King?'

'He seems to be asleep, my lady. Unfortunately all the potions and charms administered by Tok Dukun have failed to wake him up. I think he is under a curse—a powerful sleeping spell. I've heard that the only way to break this kind of spell is to kill or incapacitate the originator of the spell.'

'And we don't even know who this originator is,' said the queen despondently.

She added in a puzzled voice, 'This may sound strange coming from me, but why would they cast this spell on the king, when they had no compunction about killing the others?'

'I personally believe it could be because of an ancient taboo against spilling royal blood. Killing a king, especially from such an ancient lineage could unleash a curse, with dire consequences for the assassins themselves.'

'I see. I can very well understand the fear of such a curse, especially among those who dabble in the dark arts,' she said thoughtfully.

Maharaja Lela hesitated before suggesting, 'If Tok Dukun has failed, perhaps we should consult Tok Pawang? She is after all the most powerful among them.'

The queen nodded resignedly. 'The idea has crossed my mind before. I suppose we have no choice now. Somehow, I feel reluctant to involve her in these matters. Could you send word to her to come to the palace tomorrow evening?'

However, the investigation into the deaths of Nong Rawan and Bujang came to a standstill when a message arrived at the palace that Raja Chandra, Prince of Sri Vijaya wanted to have a private audience with Raja Perita, the next day.

His mother summoned the prince to her quarters to inform him of the visit, 'Raja Chandra wants to meet you, personally, Perita. Even though the palace is struck by tragedy, we must not disappoint the prince. We must not let the prince know what has taken place here. We need his support more than ever now. This meeting has to go well for all our sakes.'

The prince noticed that his mother's mood seemed to have lifted by this unexpected event. She no longer seemed so sombre, a faint light had returned to her eyes and she even managed a wan smile. He felt his mood lift as well and he replied, 'I will do my best, mother; for you and father, and for the kingdom. But the prince is bound to know about the two deaths. After all he has his informants in the royal palace itself.' He lowered his head and continued, 'And there are some who believe that I'm responsible for the deaths of both Rawan and Bujang.'

His mother replied, 'Deaths occur in every household, what more a palace of this size? I doubt that Raja Chandra will be unduly concerned. There are many who support you: your three friends will stand by you always, and your father and I believe completely in your innocence. Even Maharaja Lela believes that you are innocent.'

Raja Perita was genuinely surprised. He had not known that about Maharaja Lela but then few knew him; he was a man who kept his thoughts to himself. He did not reply so the queen continued, 'I want the palace to look as cheerful as possible. I've asked the palace staff to place fresh flowers in every room in polished bronze pots and the main hall is to be decorated with a magnificent kolam, surrounded by twelve silver plates filled with betel leaves, ripe areca fruits and jasmine flowers. Cook has been asked to prepare special dishes for the prince and his retinue as well, and you are to use my audience hall to entertain the prince.'

As Raja Perita rose to his feet, his mother said, 'You will try your best to be friends with the Rajaputra of Sri Vijaya, won't you? I know you prefer to spend time with your friends but this is important for us. We have to do everything in our power to impress and charm this prince and through him, his sister.'

As he got up to walk away, the queen called out to him, 'And either Maharaja Lela or I will accompany you for the discussion.'

Raja Perita hesitated for an instant. Then he surprised his mother by replying, 'No mother, I would rather that one of my friends accompany me for the discussion. It would be too awkward for me to try to charm the Rajaputra in your presence and even worse in the presence of Maharaja Lela.'

The prince returned to his chamber in a thoughtful mood. Satra was there to help him to change. Maharaja Lela had requested that he take over Bujang's duties until a replacement could be found after a month or more had passed. It would be considered indelicate to find a replacement so soon after his death. Raja Perita told Satra about his mother's plan. His friend nodded and said, 'We, that is Yala and I, will be accompanying Maharaja Lela to visit a priest tomorrow. Tok Dukun thinks he can shed some light on what's going on.'

Raja Perita nodded absent-mindedly. After a long pause he said, 'Satra, you've done a lot for me these past few months. I've decided to show my gratitude to you in a more tangible way.'

Satra was genuinely surprised. He was about to wave it away but changed his mind and said half in jest, 'Can it be true that the illustrious Raja Perita is finally showing some compassion towards his poor old friend? Are you actually going to give me something of real value?'

The prince shrugged and said, 'Open that chest over there and you can take one of my gold arm rings.'

Satra's large brown eyes lit up and he smiled in anticipation and walked to the massive sandalwood chest used to store the prince's formal clothes. Inside the large chest was a much smaller mahogany box he knew contained Raja Perita's jewellery cache. He took the small box out and carried it to the prince and placed it on the bed. He carefully opened the lid. Satra said in a surprised voice, 'There is only one arm ring inside the box, my lord. The other one is missing.'

Raja Perita sat up and peered into the mahogany box. Inside were: a heavy gold necklace, several jewelled rings and earrings, a pair of gold anklets, a pair of gold bracelets and a single arm ring. He frowned and picked up the fern-shaped arm ring in his hand. He said, 'That's odd, I remember wearing both on the night we went to the Whispering Bamboo teahouse.'

'Perhaps you dropped it that night when you were attacked at the temple,' suggested Satra.

'No,' he replied. 'I remember wearing it again the night Raja Chandra and his retinue visited us. It must have been taken by someone who has access to my chamber.'

Satra raised an eyebrow, 'You mean by Bujang?'

Raja Perita shook his head. He said, 'Bujang would never take any of my things. Could it have been her?'

'Her?' enquired Satra.

'I remember Maharaja Lela asking me if I gave any gifts to Rawan. Never mind, just take the single arm ring. I'll get another pair made easily enough.'

Satra smiled and put on the arm ring around his right arm. He said, 'I can probably get a small fortune for it from one of the rich merchants. I've been told that there is a lot of demand for royal stuff in Kota Aur. You're celebrated and famous. Everyone wants something owned by the Prince of Langkasuka.'

The prince's attention was piqued by this statement. He commented in an ironic voice, 'I guess that explains my missing silk handkerchiefs and scarves.'

* * *

The next day, Raja Chandra and his retinue arrived in the afternoon. He was accompanied by several warriors and his own palace guards. A palace retainer announced, 'His serene and ineffable highness, Rajaputra Chandra Kinnara, crown prince and heir to the throne of Sri Vijaya and his illustrious entourage are present to meet our serene and radiant Raja Perita Deria of Langkasuka.'

The prince was ushered into the queen's audience chamber by Maharaja Lela while the warriors and guards waited in the main audience hall. The Sri Vijayan prince was not alone; a striking young man arrayed in the splendid regalia of a *pratyaya*, a high-born nobleman, accompanied him.

Raja Perita and Chula were waiting for them. Both the queen and Maharaja Lela had agreed that Chula should be present for the meeting—Raja Perita sensed that in situations like this, they trusted Chula more than they trusted him. But he did not resent this fact, in fact, he was glad to have one of his friends by his side. Raja Perita and Chula stood up to greet them with all the grace and ceremony they could muster. All parties bowed ceremonially with their palms pressed together. After making the introductions, the royal chamberlain returned to his own quarters.

Looking admiringly at the beautifully decorated chamber with its ornately carved wooden windows and screens and a magnificent bronze lamp hanging from the ceiling, Rajaputra Chandra exclaimed, 'What a fabulous room! So elegant and yet festive. Somehow, I never expected that of you, Raja Perita.'

The room was now made even more enticing by masses of freshly cut flowers and betel leaves which had been carefully arranged in circular tiered bronze stands. The flowers and leaves were arranged in layers—the topmost tier was filled with fragrant pure white jasmines, the next layers were the coral jasmines, next came the pale-yellow blossoms of the *bunga tanjung*, and the lowest tier was filled with bright orange ylang-ylang flowers. The combination of flowers suffused the room with a calming and pleasing fragrance.

Raja Perita replied dryly, 'You are right, Rajaputra Chandra, my taste is much simpler. This room is in fact the queen's audience chamber but she has graciously allowed us to use it.'

Rajaputra Chandra said, 'Your mother, the Serene and Radiant Queen of Langkasuka, has an inspired and impeccable taste.'

The prince could not help feeling pleased. He said, 'Thank you; she does have an eye for colour.' He was careful not to mention that his mother chose all his clothes.

Chula cleared his throat and said, 'Rajaputra Chandra, you honour us with your presence. Shall we sit down and help ourselves to some refreshments?'

They sat down on cushions laid out on a mat and the two handmaidens helped to pour out the drinks from a bronze pitcher into silver goblets—*kafir* lime juice sweetened with honey or fresh coconut water. The prince was pleased to see that his favourite dessert, *pulut* rice cooked with coconut milk and palm sugar, had been served. Cook had also made *sri muka*, a green and white layered dessert—the top green layer made with coconut cream, sugar and *pandan* leaves, which impart a fresh green flavour which is irresistible when combined with coconut cream; while the white layer was made of *pulut* rice. They were also served fresh fruits—fresh and aromatic durian; mangoes, elegantly cut into slices; peeled *rambutans* and *lychees*. Last of all, the two handmaidens handed out betel quid to everyone, then politely bowed and gracefully withdrew from the room.

Raja Perita asked as politely as he could, 'Now that we have refreshed ourselves, perhaps you will allow me to enquire why you have honoured us with your visit?'

The Prince of Sri Vijaya said, 'We are very impressed with the hospitality shown to us by the royal court of Langkasuka. We would like to return your hospitality by inviting you, Raja Perita, and your entourage to the palace of Sri Vijaya. We are willing to loan the use of two of our ships, in order for you to make this journey.'

Both Chula and Raja Perita were surprised by this unexpected invitation. Was it just an invitation or was there something more behind it? Sometimes being invited to another kingdom could result in one being taken hostage; on the other had it could be a great diplomatic step forward.

Raja Perita hesitated about answering so Chula stepped in, 'We are deeply honoured and touched. This is truly momentous. So much so that both the prince and I have to discuss this with the King and Queen first. Allow me to assure you, that the greatest consideration will be given to your most gracious invitation.' He said this knowing full well that they probably had no choice but to accept.

The Sri Vijayan prince replied, 'Of course, we do not expect an immediate reply. We merely wanted to know what the prince's feelings were about visiting our kingdom . . .'

Raja Perita was finding it difficult to focus on what Rajaputra Chandra was saying because he felt oddly drawn to the warrior who accompanied Rajaputra Chandra. There was something disconcertingly familiar about him. When he failed to reply, Chula cleared his throat and said, 'My lord, Rajaputra Chandra is addressing you . . .'

Raja Perita turned his attention to Rajaputra Chandra and said, 'My apologies, my lord Rajaputra. Actually I'm quite looking forward to visiting Sri Vijaya.'

Chula added, 'As so am I. We have heard so many marvellous stories about the *vidhyadhara-torana*—the fairy-jewelled gateway of Sri Vijaya. People say that it is made entirely of gold and is covered with gemstones.'

Rajaputra Chandra laughed politely, 'I had no idea our *torana*'s fame has spread so far and wide—the gateway itself is carved of stone, the height of four grown men, with two stone *vidhyadhara*s standing guard at each end. The doors are actually made of heavy teak wood, but it is quite true that the *torana* is covered in beaten gold studded with gems. However, there is more to Sri Vijaya than the jewelled gateway to the royal palace. We have wonderful palaces and gardens, magnificent stone temples equal to some of yours, untouched forests teeming with colourful birds and rare beasts and crystal-clear lakes and streams you can sail down for days on end.'

Chula was captivated by his description of Sri Vijaya and was about to reply that he was keen to visit anytime but Raja Perita interrupted his friend and said to the elegant *pratyaya*, 'I feel that I have seen you before. Were you present at the incredible dance given by the beautiful dancer from Sri Vijaya? I still remember it so vividly . . . it was extraordinary.'

The young man looked abashed at being addressed so directly. At first he was at a loss for words before he finally admitted in a pleasantly husky voice, 'Yes, my lord. I was privileged to attend the wonderful feast and dance performance given in honour of the Rajaputra that night. I am always at my lord's side.'

'I would very much like to meet that marvellous dancer one day,' said Raja Perita with a wistful sigh. 'Are you quite sure you were not one of the performers that night? I'm sure I would have remembered you. I did not notice anything remarkable about the lords and ladies Rajaputra Chandra was with,' Raja Perita remarked casually.

Chula was horrified, he looked apprehensively at Raja Chandra expecting him to be mortally insulted but was astonished to see him looking completely unperturbed. However, the young lord by his side looked disconcerted.

The prince continued, 'If I may be so bold as to hazard a guess, I believe you are the dancer herself.'

Chula's jaw fell and he whispered, 'My lord, I implore you! Please restrain yourself . . .'

But then the young warrior replied, sounding much more feminine now, 'How did you guess, my lord? How could you have known that it was me?'

Raja Perita said, 'How could I forget such an unforgettable face and presence? In any case I'm usually able to see through the most elaborate disguises . . .'

This time Rajaputra Chandra interrupted him, 'You are completely right, of course, Raja Perita. We should not have attempted to deceive you. The warrior is in fact, my very own sister, Rajaputri Chaiya herself.'

This time Chula was too confused to say anything at all. However, he felt relieved that Raja Perita had been right all along; the Prince of Langkasuka had not made a fool of himself.

Raja Perita felt unusually animated, his eyes glittered with dark energy. He was not expecting to see the Princess of Sri Vijaya again and he was surprised to find how exhilarated he felt. Somehow, the darkness which seemed to have engulfed him these last few weeks evaporated in her presence. He gazed into her eyes and saw the smile which began there now playing on her petal-soft lips.

The princess said impulsively, 'I've heard so much about the magnificent gardens surrounding the palace of Langkasuka. They say that you have rare flowers and plants from all over the world growing there. Will you do me the honour of showing me around the garden, my lord.'

Raja Perita smiled and was about to reply, when he realized with dismay that the sun was still shining outside. He said gallantly, 'It will be my honour to show you around this garden, my lady but might I suggest that we wait for the sun to set first . . .'

Both Rajaputri Chaiya and Rajaputra Chandra looked at him in surprise. The princess said, 'Wait for the sun to set first? What do you mean, my lord?'

But Raja Perita was at a loss for words. He was loathed to admit that he could not bear sunlight; she would think that there was something very wrong with him . . .

Fortunately for him, Chula decided to rescue the prince. He said, 'The royal garden is in fact a "Moon Garden", my lady. The rarest and most beautiful flowers in the garden, such as the Moon Orchid, only bloom after dark.'

Rajaputri Chaiya looked impressed and said, 'Why, then we shall wait for the sun to set first! We would love to see a Moon Garden, don't we, brother?'

The handsome prince smiled at his sister, he was obviously very fond of her. He said, 'I'm truly intrigued by the idea of a Moon Garden; as you know, my name Chandra, is another name for the moon.'

Raja Perita looked pleased and relieved by the intervention by Chula. He relaxed enough to share information with his guests about what was going on in the country. Time passed so quickly that they were surprised when more food was brought in, including steamed rice cooked with coconut milk and flavoured with *pandan* leaves, grilled fish flavoured with fresh turmeric root, lemongrass and sea salt, and *gulai bayam*. Cook had decided to serve everyone the same dish, so as not to arouse suspicion. Chula wondered if everyone had the secret ingredient added to their soup. But he noticed that Raja Perita ate every drop of his *gulai bayam* while hardly eating anything else.

When dinner was over, the sun had truly set. Raja Perita turned to Rajaputri Chaiya and said, 'May I have the honour, my lady?' The princess nodded graciously and smiled. The two of them got up and walked out of the chamber into the garden. Raja Chandra and Chula followed from a discrete distance.

The princess was delighted with the royal garden and Raja Perita felt as if he was seeing it for the first time in his life. He had not noticed its subtle beauty before, although he had visited the garden almost every day since he could walk. He was also surprised to find out that out here, the perfume of the flowers seemed much stronger at night and realized that Chula may have been more correct than he had supposed when he described the garden as a 'Moon Garden'.

Rajaputri Chaiya said, 'This is so wonderful, look at the way the flowers in the trees seemed to be nodding to one another . . . and the scent from the tall trees like the *bunga tanjung* complements the flowers growing on the bushes like the jasmine and the lowest level of flowers are the orchids and shrubs.'

Raja Perita replied honestly, 'I've never actually noticed that before . . . it's wonderful to look at things through someone else's eye; somehow the old and familiar becomes new and magical . . . I'm beginning to understand that the royal gardener had a depth of knowledge about plants that no one suspected.'

The garden had been planted with several *kenanga* trees, their branches bearing masses of pure white flowers, *ylang-ylang*, which only bloom and release their scent after nightfall and the *tanjung* blossom trees. Closer to the ground were artistically grouped moonflowers, orchids and jasmines. Scented water lilies sat atop the surface of the pool, and blossomed under the moonlight.

As they walked along, they felt a bond which was almost a kinship with one another. The princess said, 'It's odd, but I feel as if we have known each other for ever . . .' as she linked her fingers with his.

He nodded quietly before saying, 'I felt it the first time when I saw you dancing.'

As the Prince of Langkasuka and the Princess of Sri Vijaya wandered in the beautiful palace garden, the full moon rose and bathed the landscape in its silvery light. The garden took on a magical air at night, with its pale, luminous flowers glowing gently in the dark, and the heady and intoxicating scents perfuming the cool night air. They fell into an almost dreamlike state as they watched the flit and flutter of ghostly moths and twinkling fireflies in the night sky.

To Chula and Rajaputra Chandra, they resembled elusive sprites wandering in the moonlight. Chula felt a weight lift off his shoulders, like the queen he realized how important this match was for Langkasuka and everyone in the kingdom. He murmured to himself, 'How wonderful they look . . . like an areca nut split into two.'

As they strolled in the garden that night, Raja Perita made an unexpected admission to Rajaputri Chaiya, 'My dear Rajaputri, I have a confession to make. I am living under a curse—I cannot even bear to be out in the sun. The light of the sun, which everyone takes for granted, is enough to kill me. Whoever chooses to marry me will be forced to live a strange life of sleeping when everyone is awake and having to be awake when the rest of the world is sleeping. I cannot force such a lonely life on anyone just for my sake.'

The princess leaned against him. She replied in a soft voice, 'It will be a small price to pay to be with you, my lord. I would rather live like this than walk under the sun forever without you.'

Raja Perita took her hands in his and turned to face her. He said, 'And the curse does not end there. There is something else . . . a vice so frightful, even you could not understand.'

But the princess placed her finger on his lips and said, 'No, do not talk of such matters, my lord. We will find a way to deal with whatever curses you may be inflicted with . . . there must be a cure.'

The prince took a deep breath, reached out for her hands and said, 'You honour me, my lady. My beloved Chaiya, will you deign to marry this poor prince? I have no caskets of precious jewels or coffers of gold to offer you, but I will strive to make you happy . . . and I do truly love you.'

The princess caught her breath, she could hardly believe what she was hearing. She finally replied, 'There is no one I would rather spend my life with, my lord, Perita.'

They gazed into each other's eyes, spellbound. Giving in to an impulse, he bent down to kiss her but she pushed him away gently, whispering, 'Remember that we are being watched.'

The prince came to himself with a start and said regretfully, 'It slipped my mind.' Then he said impulsively, 'We should go somewhere else then . . . where we can be alone. Hmmm, no visit to Kota Aur is complete without a visit to our famous teahouses. It's only late evening, we still have plenty of time to sample a cup of hot tea and sweet cakes.'

She looked at him in surprise but also with anticipation, 'Teahouses? I've never been to one! Is it safe?'

His eyes glowed and he smiled mischievously, 'You're dressed like a battle-ready warrior. What could happen to us?' He caught hold of her hand and pulled her towards the back gate of the garden. The two of them slipped out before Chula and Rajaputra Chandra realized what was happening. The prince gasped, 'He's taking my sister out of the palace grounds! We have to follow them!'

Chula turned towards Rajaputra Chandra and said, 'I believe we have a treaty to sign.'

Rajaputra Chandra nodded and was about to reply when he said in an alarmed voice, 'Quickly, we have to follow them before they slip out of sight!'

The Story of the Temple Maiden

While Raja Perita and Chula were entertaining the prince and princess of Sri Vijaya; Maharaja Lela and Tok Dukun walked out of the palace grounds into Kota Aur. They were accompanied by Satra, Yala and two palace guards. Led by Tok Dukun, they had to take a long and winding path through the outskirts of Kota Aur to reach the small temple. The journey took them almost an hour and the sun was already low in the sky when they reached the temple.

Maharaja Lela was relieved when they arrived at their destination—he was not used to long walks in the afternoon. He was pleasantly surprised to see how clean and well-kept the temple and its surroundings appeared to be. Even the flower garden was well tended and he noticed a frangipani tree near the temple and several bushes of jasmine growing in the nearby garden. There was also a large mango tree growing at the back of the temple, heavily laden with fruits and a banana grove at the edge of the forest.

An old man in a white cloth came out to greet them. His long grey hair was tied in a bun behind his head but he was clean shaven. They greeted each other courteously and the priest invited them to be seated on the raised floor of the temple. They were served betel quid, as well as bananas, sliced mangoes and fresh coconut water as a preamble before Tok Dukun introduced the members of the group to the priest. He also briefly explained the purpose of their visit.

Maharaja Lela said, 'Allow me to elaborate. A year ago, our prince was attacked by a creature in a ruined temple; she was described as a beautiful young woman with dark skin. She apparently wanted to drink his blood but we were fortunate that his friends rescued the prince and Tok Dukun here managed to save his life. However, we have not been able to locate this temple, despite searching all over Kota Aur and its outskirts. And oddly enough no one seems to know its whereabouts. But we thought that was the end of it until a few nights ago when two servants from the palace seemed to have been attacked by the same creature. They passed away, unfortunately, their body drained of blood.'

Tok Dukun added, 'I thought initially that it was a *pontianak*, a female demon created when a young woman dies during childbirth. But this seems unlikely as the prince is a strong and skilled warrior and the other two victims were young and strong. One of them was a servant of the prince, in fact.'

The priest said, 'I've heard about the prince being attacked by a female demon some time ago. It reminds me of stories I've heard in my old country; stories of a demon known as the *vetal*. The *vetal* is a vampire, it is created when a demon takes possession of a dead body and reanimates it. The *vetal* are extremely strong and they can move very quickly, sometimes faster than the eyes can see. They hide in the dark and the shadows of the night. They are also very perceptive with an uncanny understanding of human nature and some say, the ancient ones can even read and control our minds.'

Maharaja Lela asked, 'Do you think there is a *vetal* in our midst?'

The priest said, 'It is more than possible from what you have just told me . . . there is an old story I heard as a child. In my old village in Bharat, people tell the story of a beautiful young woman, who was a handmaiden of a dark goddess.'

The priest paused to draw his breath before continuing, 'But misfortune did not spare the woman. One night she was abducted by a group of brigands from a distant village. These men practised blood sacrifice and offered her to their own blood-thirsty goddess. When she was dying, legend say that her own goddess appeared to her and offered her some of her own blood. The handmaiden came back to life and killed all the men who sacrificed her by drinking their blood.'

By now, even the sceptical Maharaja Lela was listening to him with bated breath. The priest continued, 'The men did not know that they had unleashed a curse by killing the handmaiden.'

Yala asked with bated breath, 'You mean that the goddess turned her into a *vetal*?'

The priest nodded sombrely, 'It would seem so . . . the handmaiden or rather the creature she had turned into started to prey on the villagers. When the rest of the villagers realized what had happened, they tried to capture her. She had to flee into the forests and hide in caves in the hills. It was not an easy life for her and she knew that she had to flee to a new land.'

Maharaja Lela asked curiously, 'But how did she come to Langkasuka?'

The priest replied, 'According to the story, she came to this country in a trading ship a long time ago. I am not sure exactly how it happened; all I know is that the people around her started dying . . . they drove her into the forest and trapped her in an old temple there. All the priests cast a binding spell so that she is always bound to the temple; she can never leave the place.'

Maharaja Lela looked grave when he heard the priest's story. He said, 'This story makes me very concerned because if it is true that the woman is bound to the temple and can never leave it; this can only mean that she could not have killed the two palace attendants and there is another *vetal* in Kota Aur!'

The priest nodded and added, 'There could be more than one or even two *vetal* in Kota Aur! Fortunately for us, she cannot create too many as it drains her own life force.'

Everyone looked horrified. Maharaja Lela asked tentatively, 'How do we kill this creature?'

The priest said, 'The method is fairly simple; you can cut off the creature's head or burn it with fire. The difficulty lies in identifying and capturing a *vetal* for they have an uncanny understanding of human nature and have the ability to move in the blink of an eye and hide among the shadows . . . they are also extremely, supernaturally strong.'

Yala asked unexpectedly, 'Apart from an acute aversion to sunlight, does the *vetal* have any other weaknesses?'

The priest looked surprised at the question. He thought for a while before replying, 'Indeed, the *vetal* has an acute aversion to sunlight and must remain hidden in dark places during daylight hours. The *vetal* must sleep during the day and roam the night—it is the weakest when asleep, close to death. I understand that there is a special ritual which when performed can bind the will of a *vetal* to a human.'

Both Satra and Maharaja Lela looked disturbed by this answer. Satra felt compelled to ask, 'But the *vetal* are not necessarily evil or driven to evil acts?'

The priest looked surprised by this question, 'As a matter of fact, you are right. They are usually controlled by the spirit which possesses them, but not all are driven to evil acts. Some protect their villages from harm. They are also bound by truth and may swear allegiance to the one whom they have a profound respect or love.'

Maharaja Lela looked grave. As twilight was fast approaching, he thanked the priest as the group took their leave and decided to hurry home. They dropped Tok Dukun off in his house in Kota Aur and managed to reach the palace grounds just before the last evening light faded in the sky.

A few nights later, Maharaja Lela woke up with a start. His hair was standing on end. He had heard a movement in the room. It was a mere rustle but he could not deny its presence; his racing heart told him that he had not imagined it. Then he saw it from the corner of his eyes . . . a dark shadow spreading its tentacles towards him. His heart froze in terror and cold sweat broke out on his forehead. He tried to call out but his voice would not come out. He gathered his courage and willed himself to calm down and his hand reached out for the dagger he always kept under his pillow.

A cold hard voice said, 'It's too late, my lord, Maharaja Lela . . . you know that I will always be stronger and faster than you.'

Maharaja Lela only managed to gasp out, 'So it was you all along. I had my suspicions.'

The voice sneered, 'You are too clever for your own good, my lord! You should have minded your own business instead of trying to find out the truth about those two miserable slaves.'

Maharaja Lela managed to gasp out, 'They may be servants but they are also human beings after all . . . aaargh!' before a second shadow solidified, and grabbed him by the shoulders. Maharaja Lela felt sharp claw-like nails digging into his shoulders. He tried to cry out for help but sharp fangs sank into his neck.

Then the assassin saw the gold bracelet resting on top of the mahogany box at the side of the bed. The killer picked it up before vanishing from the chamber.

Maharaja Lela's servant found his body the next morning. His bed was soaked in blood and his throat had been ripped. Maharaja Lela, one of the highest nobles in the land had been murdered in the foulest manner.

The queen was horrified to hear about Maharaja Lela's death and ordered the palace to go into mourning, hoping that this death would be the last.

The turmoil in the palace was mirrored in the prince's mind. Raja Perita brooded about the horrific turn of events. Maharaja Lela was dead; there was no one to defend his name. More appalling was the fact that the royal chamberlain was the father of one of his closest friends.

Chula was at first in deep shock over the death of his father, especially because of the horrible way he died. He had never been especially close to his father, who spent most of his time in the palace, where he had his own chambers. Somehow his father's death created a feeling of deep regret which surprised him. He retreated to his mother's house and remained in seclusion. He was inconsolable for days and refused to talk to anyone. Satra and Yala paid him a visit at his mother's residence—a spacious and elegant timber house just outside the palace grounds. They met outside his house and Yala's eyes caught the beautiful fern-shaped arm bracelet Satra was wearing; he recognized it as belonging to the prince. He remarked in a voice laden with irony, 'I see that you have found favour in the eyes of our prince.'

Satra replied without affectation, 'I have been doing a lot of work for the prince recently. Anyway Raja Perita has changed since the bad luck which befell him.'

Yala said, 'But you don't have the other one, though.'

At that moment, the front door opened and they were ushered in by the maid. They were warmly welcomed by his mother. The maid offered them a tray of betel quid and fresh fruits; they declined the fruits but accepted the betel quid and proceeded to chew them.

Chula came out of his chamber to greet them. He looked pale and drawn and had dark rings under his eyes. He was dressed entirely in white, the colour of mourning. After greeting each other politely, Chula invited them into his chamber. They sat down on the finely woven mat in the middle of the room.

After a period of silence, Satra said, 'Chula, we came to share your burden. We are so very sorry about what happened to your esteemed father, the Maharaja Lela. We can't imagine how you must be feeling now. No one ever expected something like this could happen in the palace itself.'

A look of pain crossed his face but Chula pulled himself together. He responded, 'I never thought that I would actually miss my father so much. We never got to see much of him. As everyone knows, he gave his life to his duties and spent most of his time at the palace.'

An unexpectedly regretful voice said, 'We can never tell how much we are going to miss someone, until they are gone.' It was Yala who spoke and everyone looked at him in surprise. It was unlike Yala to display emotions such as disappointment or unhappiness, least of all regret.

Chula asked hesitantly, 'So the prince is not here.'

Satra replied sadly, 'My lord, Raja Perita, wanted to visit you, really he did . . . You know that he cares for you deeply. He asked how you were keeping several times but the queen prohibited him. The prince is not allowed to leave the palace as the queen believed that he may be in danger.'

Chula nodded, 'Of course. I only hope that he is keeping well. After all, we love him and we live to serve him.'

Satra said in quiet anger, 'The only consolation is that the spate of deaths seemed to have ended. I just wish things would go back to what they were. Why did we ever have to meet that horrible creature on that accursed night.'

While they were talking, the ornate bay windows at the back of the room suddenly opened and they were shocked to see Raja Perita standing outside. The prince said in a nonchalant voice, 'Aren't you going to invite me in, Lord Chula?'

Chula finally found his voice. He said in a broken voice, 'Please come in, my lord, Perita. I thought I would never see you again.'

Satra gasped, 'My lord, what are you doing here? Your mother has forbidden you from leaving the palace.'

Raja Perita strode into the chamber before replying ironically, 'You can't expect me to obey my mother all the time, Satra. Remember, I'm supposed to be wilful, unruly and downright defiant.'

All three rose to their feet to greet him. In an unexpected gesture, the prince walked towards Chula and embraced him. Chula looked surprised and touched at the same time. He stammered, 'This is so . . . unexpected, my lord.'

Raja Perita released him and held him at arm's length. He looked Chula in the eyes and said, 'I can't allow you to grieve by yourself, old friend . . . I know that people are blaming me for Maharaja Lela's death. I don't really care about what people are saying but I can't allow you to continue thinking that I ever had anything to do with it.'

They sat down on the mat in a tight circle to talk. Raja Perita said, 'We have to find out who is behind all these killings. Maybe if we share our thoughts, we can pool our knowledge and get to the bottom of this sinister plot.'

After a brief silence, Chula said in a sombre voice, 'I guess my father came too close to the truth . . . he must have found out who the killer really was, and had to be silenced.'

Everyone nodded in agreement. Yala said, 'Whoever it was, knows his way around the palace. So I think we can assume that either he works in the palace as a guard or a servant, or he could even be a nobleman.'

Satra agreed with Yala, 'Yes, it must be someone very familiar with the palace. And I think it could also be a woman, seeing as how the prince was attacked by a female demon.'

Chula said, 'It has to be a woman with extraordinary strength and skill as she managed to overcome Bujang and the Maharaja Lela. My father may be old but he was quite strong for his age.'

Yala suddenly turned towards the prince and asked, 'What about the Rajaputeri of Sri Vijaya? Will the engagement take place after such a tragic incident?'

Raja Perita looked surprised at his question. He hesitated before replying, 'I haven't actually given it much thought. I mean I think of her all the time, but it never occurred to me to consider the possibility that the engagement would be broken because of this.' He broke off and looked concerned.

Chula pulled himself up and said in a decisive voice, 'The engagement with the Rajaputeri of Sri Vijaya has to take place, no matter what has happened. My father would have wanted it.'

The four friends talked for a while longer before the prince decided to take his leave, he did not want his mother to find out that he had defied her by leaving the palace. He was followed by Yala. Satra decided to stay behind and keep the still distraught Chula company.

When Raja Perita returned to the palace, he was surprised to find his mother waiting for him in his chamber.

'Mother! Are you all right? Is anything wrong?' His voice expressed his concern. His mother never broke decorum unless she was extremely concerned.

'There is something I have to tell you, Perita. Maharaja Lela advised me to keep this a secret but now that he is dead, I can no longer keep it to myself. I wish I had told you this earlier. It's about your father.'

The prince did not say anything. He could tell from the apprehension in his mother's face and voice that it was something important and difficult for her to reveal to him. He sat down on the mat, his ankles crossed and his hands resting on his knees, and faced his mother.

His mother took a deep breath and launched into speech. 'Your father is not really in seclusion. When Rawan was attacked, someone put a spell on him. He fell into a deathlike trance and neither the magic of Tok Dukun nor Tok Pawang could break the spell.'

Raja Perita turned pale. He was too shocked to say anything.

The queen continued, 'Maharaja Lela felt it was best to keep this hidden from the rest of the court as well as the people. He told everyone the King was in seclusion and as your father had done this before, no one thought to question him. We had to keep it a secret, the kingdom is already strained from recent events.'

Raja Perita finally managed to gasp, 'Mother! Why didn't you tell me this before?'

'My son, you were already so troubled. You were fighting for your sanity . . . I couldn't burden you further. I admit, I also wanted you to be happy enough to be able to charm the Sri Vijayan Princess. We really thought we could break the spell and rouse him before anyone found out anything.'

The prince sighed in exasperation. He rose to his feet and strode out of the chamber. He said, 'Is it any surprise that no one trusts me when even my own mother is unable to trust me with the truth about my father? You should have trusted me enough to tell me the truth, mother!'

'Perita, please try to understand! Don't walk away from me,' but her pleas fell on deaf ears.

The queen looked out of her window and saw the prince slipping away out of the palace gates. She sighed in resignation but she had expected it to happen anyway. She picked up her silk shawl, wrapped it around her and walked silently out of the palace and into the moon garden. She headed straight for the little rock pool at the far end of the garden. It had a stand of bamboo at the edge, but these were not the giant *buluh betong*, they were ornamental bamboo plants. The moon reflected into the pool and the gentle rustling of the bamboo leaves made her feel melancholy. She sighed to herself without realizing it. But she gathered her resolve and walked straight into the bamboo patch. The queen knelt on the ground and placed both palms of her hand on the earth. She chanted an incantation and called out: 'I summon you, my birth mother, the silver haired yakshi of the bamboo grove! I summon you!'

But there was no response and the queen sensed that the yakshi was nowhere near. She called out, more insistently, 'I summon you to appear before me, here and now! I have seen your face through my son's eyes, and I know your true nature! You cannot deny my call!'

There was still no response so the queen used all her will power to drain the life force from the bamboo plants which slowly started to wither. Bit by bit the bamboo started turning brown, spreading like a line of fire all the way down the hill and through the fingers of bamboo which went all the way into the ancient forest. As she did so, her eyes burned red, like live coals and her hair seemed to move as if alive; the silver streak of hair shone in the moon light.

'Enough!' a cold and silvery voice suddenly echoed through the grove. The queen looked up, startled, and saw a tall slender woman standing among the grove. Although she had seen her in the vision, it was startling to actually meet her in person. Her eyes burned like fire in her pale face, which was framed by a cascade of long silver hair. She looked young, even younger than the queen herself. The yakshi continued coldly, 'Why have you summoned me, Princess of the Bamboo?'

The queen entreated the yakshi, 'We may have never met but you are still my mother! I need your assistance and advice; my son is under threat. A dark creature has turned him into a blood drinker and a slave of the night; he is unable to walk in the sun any more. And there are those who believe that he is a murderer and wish to kill my only child. I need to help him; I need to find a *pawang* powerful enough to cure him.'

She was upset and surprised to see the yakshi laugh mirthlessly. The yakshi replied, 'Why are you looking for a *pawang* when you are the most powerful shaman in the entire kingdom, and probably in all the other kingdoms too? You have yakshi blood in your veins and you wield more magic than any *pawang*!'

The queen was stunned by this revelation. For a moment she was speechless while she tried to grasp what the yakshi had just told her. She said, 'Yes, but I do not know how to use my power! I want to know how to save my son! What is it that I must do?'

This time it was the yakshi who was silent. After a moment she said, 'You have to give him your tears . . . the tears of a yakshi have a potent magic. Unfortunately most of us are unable to cry, humans see us as cold and heartless but we are neither good nor evil, just like nature. But your human emotions give you this ability. Your tears have immense healing powers and will give him the ability to walk in the sun, at least for short periods of time. But it is painful if not impossible for a yakshi to weep, as I'm sure you know; to us it is equivalent to giving blood.'

Then she broke off several pieces of bamboo and waved her hand slowly over them while whispering an incantation. Magical energy in the form of green light swirled around the bamboo stems, which slowly knitted together and fused until they formed a seamless bowl. The yakshi pulled out an impossibly long strand of her silver hair and placed it in the bowl. The hair coiled by itself inside the bowl. Then she handed the bamboo container to the queen and said, 'Use this container to collect your tears; but while you weep you must feel joy not sorrow, for the tears of joy are the most potent of all.'

The queen gratefully took the container from her hands and forced herself to weep into it. It was painful just as the yakshi had said but she tried her best to remember all the happy moments of her life, such as her carefree childhood in the hills with Tok Batin and even the difficult moments which ultimately brought her happiness: her marriage to the king and the birth of her only child . . . She wept until she had no more tears and blood started seeping from her eyes. By now the streak of silver running down her head had widened until it covered almost half her head. An overwhelming feeling of tiredness threatened to overcome her.

The yakshi intervened in time, 'Stop! You have poured enough of your *semangat* into the vassal. It is time to stop weeping. You cannot help your son with your own death, you need to teach him how to live, not die. Here let me seal it for you.' She waved her hand over the bamboo container while whispering an incantation and the bowl sealed itself. She said, 'Give this to your son; the seal is magical and can only be opened by the one it is intended for. It is time for me to leave now.' And she turned to walk away.

The queen called out to her, 'Thank you, mother! Please let me how I can ever repay you.'

The yakshi turned around, her face looking drawn and pale. She said, 'I sense that another heinous act has been committed, an act which has disturbed the rice spirit itself. At the next harvest, you are to perform the ritual of summoning the rice spirit as your old Tok Batin taught you in the past. Otherwise there will be more misery in the kingdom and people will start to encroach on my land.' She paused and added, 'And remember to tell your son that he is also part yaksha; I have awakened the ability in him to swallow the *semangat* of others.'

Tok Pawang walked slowly into the harvested rice fields, her dark piercing eyes gazing unwaveringly into the gloom of the deserted fields. Three months after the harvest season, it was time to appease the rice spirit again. She was carrying a large tray woven from dried *mengkuang* leaves and bound by bamboo. Inside the tray were nine bundles of slender purple sugar cane, nine betel leaf quid, nine bundles of jasmine flowers and a bowl of sticky rice—tinted yellow with turmeric.

She walked from one field to another, uttering an incantation and placing the offerings in one corner of the field until she came to the ninth. Here she placed the bowl of sticky rice and the last offering. Tok Pawang uttered the incantation for the ninth time. She caught her breath when she saw a faint light shimmering in the distance. It was coming from a person who was slowly approaching her. The figure of a slender young girl with long unbound hair materialized out of the darkness. Tok Pawang gasped in astonishment, her heart was racing with joy—it was the rice spirit herself! Tok Pawang had only seen her once before in her life; when she herself was a young woman and had to summon the rice spirit for the first time. It was an image she would never forget and it had confirmed her calling as the shaman of Bujang Valley. The figure came closer but a look akin to distress suddenly appeared on her beautiful face. The rice spirit whispered, 'Tok Pawang, this is the last time I will see you. Farewell, old friend!' before it faded from sight.

Tok Pawang felt fear grip her and she heard a faint sound behind her. She turned around to face her enemy and said grimly, 'I am not afraid, come out and show yourself.'

The creature showed itself in the pale light of the moon. The shaman planted her feet firmly on the ground and quietly took out the small harvest knife she always carried with her. The creature snarled and sprang at her but Tok Pawang slashed it with her knife. It howled in pain. The shaman would have escaped with her life if not for the person who slashed her throat from behind. But she still managed to turn around and slash one arm.

The next morning, a group of boys came across a dead body in an empty rice field at the edge of the forest. It was Tok Pawang of Bujang Valley. Just like Rawan, Bujang and Maharaja Lela, her throat had been ripped and her body was drained of blood. Her violent murder sent a shudder of horror and fear through the entire kingdom, even more than Maharaja Lela's death could. Rice land was sacred; violence and death were taboo in rice fields. People whispered that the rice spirit will abandon the land and future harvests will fail, bringing misery and the threat of starvation.

Rumours also spread of a dark supernatural creature stalking the palace and roaming the streets and lanes of Kota Aur, pouncing on unwary people and draining their body of blood. People whispered that the creature was horrible looking with long unkempt black hair and red eyes. Fear seeped slowly through the kingdom.

An Ancient Curse

The palace of Langkasuka was in turmoil: Maharaja Lela, the man who saw to the smooth running of the palace was dead. The palace was officially in a state of mourning but there was the engagement ceremony of the Prince of Langkasuka to the Princess of Sri Vijaya to be arranged. It was an event that the queen was determined to see through.

After consulting with Raja Perita and Chula, who had taken over his father's post as Maharaja Lela, the queen fixed an auspicious date for the engagement. It was to be a subdued and quiet affair, known only to a handful of people closest to the prince and princess. To be on the safe side, only Rajaputra Chandra and Rajaputri Chaiya knew the actual date of the engagement on the Sri Vijayan camp.

But Raja Perita knew it would not be long before events came to a head. When Chula came to see him about the Rajaputri Chaiya's preference for food and clothing, the prince said in a subdued voice, 'Somehow, I have a feeling that my engagement to the Rajaputri is not going to take place.'

It was one of the few times in his life that the fiercely proud prince looked dejected; the aura of energy and self-assurance which seemed second nature to him was fading. Chula wished that he knew how to console him. He replied, 'You are overly pessimistic, my lord. We have taken all the necessary steps and precautions, and I will do everything in my power to make sure that it will take place!' He tried to sound as optimistic as he could.

The prince replied enigmatically, 'I sensed that there is someone among us who does not want to see me happy.'

The day of reckoning came sooner than he expected. The night before his engagement to Rajaputri Chaiya, Raja Perita woke up with a jolt. He was immediately alert and sat up with his dagger clenched in his hand. He sensed that something was wrong, the air was charged with tension and dark energy as if a storm was brewing in the distance.

He was surprised when his mother suddenly slipped into the room. She gave a start when she realized that he was already up. His mother noticed that his eyes glowed in the dark, like cat's eyes. He sensed his mother's anxiety and asked quietly, 'What is it, mother? What's happening?'

She whispered, 'The people are gathering at the palace gates carrying torches. They mean to set fire to the palace in order to capture you.'

Looking at her closely, he was shocked to see that most of her hair had turned silver. 'Mother, what happened to your hair? The last time I saw you, you did not have so much grey hair, and you look so tired.' His voice sounded deeply concerned.

The queen said, 'Don't worry about my hair and looks, Perita. The palace may be under siege.'

He said with a sigh, 'I was afraid something like this might happen. How many of them are there, mother? Can't the guards take care of them?'

The prince did not wait for his mother to reply. He quickly got out of bed and looked out of the tall wooden bay windows of his chamber. He could see faint shadows moving around the courtyard below, a few of them carrying lighted torches. Beyond the palace walls were masses of glowing silhouettes, among the trees. To his preternatural eyes, the people stood out in the dark like red silhouettes while the torch they were carrying burnt through the darkness with an intense yellow-white flame. Raja Perita realized that the guards were no longer at their post. Fear made him short-tempered. He snarled under his breath, 'The cowardly churls! They have abandoned us.'

His mother replied in a low voice, 'I just don't understand how this could happen, Perita. It seems that the entire kingdom has risen against us.'

The prince turned towards his mother and said grimly, 'The guards can't hold back the entire town and countryside! We have no choice but to leave Kota Aur, at least for a while. I don't want any harm to come to you or father because of me.'

His mother said calmly, 'No, we will stay behind. Your father and I, together with the *bangsawan* who are still loyal to us. Your father is in no condition to travel and I have to stay behind to take care of him. I know the crowd will not harm him because the people have always held him in high regard. Also it is taboo to spill royal blood. Please go, my son. We will be safe.'

He clenched his fists and said fiercely, 'I can't leave you behind, mother. It's my duty to protect you.'

His mother reached out and held his hands in hers. She whispered urgently, 'My son, listen! You have to live for us. Your father and I can take care of ourselves as long as you are safe. Your only chance is to flee! Even now they are at the palace gate.'

He relented, he knew that his mother was right—the people would not harm his father or his mother; she was the revered Bamboo Princess; the only one who could summon the rice spirit now that Tok Pawang was gone. He quickly changed into his hunting clothes while his mother folded a mat and an extra set of clothes and placed them in his blanket which she knotted into a bag. She also gave him a smaller leather pouch with the words, 'There are gold and silver coins in the leather pouch; enough money to last for many months.'

She paused and took out the bamboo container she had hidden in the folds of her clothes. She handed it to him with the words, 'The bamboo holds the essence of the yakshi and also some of my essence; when you drink it, it will fully awaken the yaksha magic in you. You will be able to walk under the sun, at least for short periods of time and you will be able to swallow the *semangat* of other beings. Remember this is both a curse and a gift; do not allow unbridled emotions to take hold of you.'

'Mother, what have you done? Is that why your hair has turned white?' he asked, his voice sounding anguished.

She brushed him aside with the words, 'Now is not the time to argue with me, Perita! You have to hurry. Take the hidden passage in the palace and escape through the gate at the end of the garden. Your friends are waiting there.'

She placed her cold hands on his face and said, 'Leave now, Perita! Do not allow yourself to be caught.'

He said darkly, 'I'm both yaksha and vampire, mother. No one can see me, when I choose not to be seen.'

The prince embraced his mother and said farewell to her before leaving the palace swiftly and silently. He did not see his mother weeping silently as he left. He made his way through the garden, blending into the shadows of the trees until he reached the hidden gate which led to Kota Aur. As his mother had said, Chula, Satra and Yala were waiting for him. They looked relieved to see him and quickly escorted him through the gate. They were dressed in the simple clothes of the townspeople, in order to attract as little attention as possible. Each of them carried a cloth bag with food and a few essential items. They could hear the loud cries of the crowd which had surrounded the front of the palace as walked silently towards the back streets of Kota Aur.

The prince was in a sombre mood. He said, 'I'm grateful to the three of you for being faithful to me. But the sun is rising and I need to find shelter soon. As you well know, I cannot tolerate the sun.'

Yala said quickly, 'Then we should make our way into the forest outside of Kota Aur as quickly as possible. The good thing is that everyone is gathered in front of the palace so no one will be looking for us in town.'

Chula looked doubtful at Yala's suggestion. He said, 'I feel that the forest is too far away; the sun will be above the horizon by the time we arrive. We need a place to rest nearby.'

They continued walking as quickly as they could while talking under their breath. Then Satra had an idea. He said, 'I know a place where we can hide. There is a little-known temple just outside of Kota Aur. Yala and I followed the late Maharaja Lela there, several days ago. The priest is friendly and from another land. He will not mind providing us with shelter at the temple.'

Satra and Yala led them to the little temple without much difficulty. The sun was already peeping over the horizon when they arrived. Raja Perita glanced anxiously at the rising sun. The priest was already up and performing his morning rituals when they arrived. He turned slightly pale and looked apprehensive when he saw the prince but he welcomed them into his home, nevertheless.

The priest led the prince inside the wooden house which served as his dwelling, followed by the three friends. The priest told them, 'I need to speak alone to the prince.'

They were surprised by this request and refused to budge at first. Chula said firmly, 'One of us must always be by the side of the prince.'

But Raja Perita looked at the priest closely in the eyes and said, 'It's all right, I trust him. Please leave us alone for a while.'

When they left his side, the priest said, 'You bear the marks of being attacked by the handmaiden of the dark goddess, and yet you are not fully a *vetal* yet. Perhaps it is because you are still alive. Very few ever survive such an attack.'

Raja Perita replied, 'I survived because I am part yaksha . . . my grandmother was a powerful yakshi with silver hair.'

The priest looked astonished by his answers. After a pause he nodded and said, 'Of course, a yaksha might be able to steal the life force of even a *vetal*. Perhaps you will be able to destroy her once and for all. Did your mother teach you how to draw the memories of a person?'

Raja Perita said slowly, 'Yes, I think so . . .Why is this important?'

The priest replied grimly, 'It is important because the secret to vanquishing her may lie in her own memory.'

The priest offered him what looked like a bowl of milk and said, 'Drink this . . . It will help you to sleep while the sun is up. Meanwhile, I will perform the necessary rites to sanctify your weapons so that you may accomplish the task ahead; remember that most supernatural beings are undone by iron!'

When the priest left the hut, the prince had fallen into a deep sleep. The priest told the other three, 'You may rest here in the temple for the day but you have to find another place to hide after sunset. I cannot keep the prince here for longer than a day or your presence will be known.'

They were provided with simple food, including rice, lentils and bananas. They had no difficulty falling asleep as they had been up all night. The priest woke them up by sunset and they set off on their journey.

The Traitor

This time it was Yala who led them. He seemed to know exactly where he was going and took them along a path which looked oddly familiar. The faint scent of champaka drifted in the breeze, and the prince felt slightly ill. He remarked softly, 'The scent of champaka always makes me feel uneasy.'

Chula replied, 'We do not sense anything, my lord. Neither champaka nor any other flower. Perhaps the heat is too oppressive.' He looked at the prince with concern.

Yala laughed softly and said, 'My lord can detect scents that we can only imagine. To our beloved prince, the scent of champaka will always presage danger.'

The prince caught his breath and a shadow seemed to fall over his face. How did Yala know? He had never told anyone about his aversion to champaka and the fact that he had sensed it in the palace, on the night Rawan had been killed. It all added up in his mind—the fact that it was Yala who first suggested that they visit the unknown teahouse that fateful night, his knowledge of Angkor politics, the jewellery found in Rawan's possession—Satra was too poor and he was clearly not interested in the maiden—while Chula was too aloof to ever pursue a palace handmaiden. And he sensed that Yala was hiding something underneath his long sleeved tunic. When did he ever wear long sleeves? He stopped in his tracks, turned towards his friend and said softly, 'So it was you, Yala, who betrayed us.'

Both Chula and Satra looked shocked. They stared at the prince and then at Yala. Chula remained silent but Satra protested, 'Yala? But that's impossible, my lord. Yala is of royal blood; he is your own cousin. He would never betray us!'

Raja Perita continued, 'Yes, it's Yala; my own royal cousin who broke our covenant. I knew it must be someone high born, with intimate knowledge of the palace and able to enter the royal quarters at will.'

Yala had turned as pale as a ghost. He snapped, 'You have no right to accuse me of treachery . . . you arrogant, selfish, cur.'

Chula interjected, 'Bite your tongue, Yala! The prince may be unwell but that does not give you the right to call him a cur.'

Then he turned towards Raja Perita and said imploringly, 'This is not the time to create dissension among your truest friends, my lord! We need to stand together when we face our enemy.'

Raja Perita replied, 'Chula, he betrayed himself when he mentioned that the smell of champaka always presages danger for me! No one knew this about me, not you and not even Satra. And have you forgotten? He was the one who suggested that we visit the Whispering Bamboo teahouse so many months ago.'

Chula and Satra were too shocked to say anything.

Yala turned pale with fear and rage. He gripped the hilt of his weapon and spat out, 'It seems that you possess more intelligence than anyone gave you credit for, my lord! Who would have guessed that the pampered Prince of Langkasuka was actually observing the people around him!'

'Well, you can blame yourself for this as well, Yala. Because of my dark gifts, I share some of the pain and sorrow of the people around me . . . and I sense you hide a wound underneath your long sleeves. People did say Tok Pawang managed to wound her assailant,' the prince replied.

Yala replied sardonically, 'That's strange because I feel even less than I used to. In fact, I now feel free from all those emotional encumbrances.'

Raja Perita said, 'How dare you! You killed the poor girl and then took the life of an innocent young man, my own servant. Yala, they had the right to live! And . . . you killed Tok Pawang to turn the people against me? You realized that the people were not overly concerned about the death of two palace retainers, but the death of Tok Pawang of Bujang Valley would push them into hysteria . . . I couldn't understand what was going on at first but then I remembered the smell of champaka. It was all around the demon's grove and I sensed it when I met Rawan that night, but I realize now that I had detected it much earlier. On that night before I was attacked, the scent was on you, Yala!'

For once, Yala remained silent. The prince added bitterly, 'I wish I had the words to express the intense disappointment I feel right now, Yala.'

Satra finally spoke up, 'Why Yala? Why would you do such a thing? You were the one who had the most promise and the brightest future.'

Yala almost wailed, 'I was in love with Rawan but she turned me away. She had some idea in her head that our lord, Perita, would actually marry her, the silly fool! She said that she had discovered his secret . . . can you imagine?'

Satra said with dawning comprehension, 'And I suppose Bujang must have seen you and confronted you about it, and you had to silence him as well.'

Yala almost laughed, 'He actually had the nerve to challenge me to a duel . . . He can't even hold a *keris* properly!'

Chula, who had been silent since the prince mentioned the string of murders, said quietly, 'And my father? I suppose, you killed my father, Maharaja Lela, one of the highest nobles in the land because he was getting too close to the truth.'

Yala spat out angrily, 'I didn't want to kill him but Maharaja Lela was too clever for his own good. He suspected I had a hand in Rawan's and Bujang's death. He could never mind his own business; that old scoundrel!'

Chula had turned pale with fury. He raised his voice in uncharacteristic rage, 'You murderous demon! You took my father's life just to escape banishment!' and charged at him with his *keris*, but Raja Perita grabbed his arm and stopped him. He said in a controlled voice, 'Chula, he is too strong for you. There is something unnatural about Yala—not quite human but not vampire either. Let me deal with him.'

But Chula wrenched his hand away and wailed, 'He killed my father . . . how can I let him get away with it?'

The prince reminded him, 'Remember the ancient beliefs about spilling royal blood? Even if you only wound him, you might unleash a curse on yourself. He is the son of my father's sister and only I can take his life.'

The prince paused and continued, 'Besides, it's all a lie. Everything Yala said is a lie. He was never in love with Rawan; even if this was true, he would have known all along that I would never marry her and she would have accepted him anyway. And he did not kill Maharaja Lela to cover up the two murders . . . not entirely. Chula, your father probably guessed the real reason behind the murders, which baffled everyone else. It was the murder of Tok Pawang—which seemed unconnected at that time—but now made me realize that it was a plot to sow discord and pin the deaths on me . . . After all, rumours were spreading among the people that their prince was a monster . . .'

'You mean, it was a plot to bring down the royal house so that Yala could ascend the throne of Langkasuka!' Satra said in disgust. Chula gritted his teeth and bowed his head. His emotions were boiling and tears of rage and grief spilled from his eyes. But he had grown up being trained to control his emotions and forced himself to calm down. He would let his father down even more by getting himself killed.

Yala said grimly, 'Bujang may not know how to fight but I do!' He drew his *sundang* and flew at the prince with astonishing speed. Chula and Satra stepped back. This was a fight between the prince and Yala. The prince avoided his blow by jumping out of the way with uncanny speed. He drew his own sword and flew towards Yala. He struck a blow but Yala parried it with his sword. He kicked the prince in the stomach and sent him flying across the path. The prince hit a tree with a thud before landing on his feet. He snarled and waited for Yala to attack again. Yala raised his *sundang* and lunged at him. Raja Perita focused all his mind and willed time to slow down. He could see Yala approaching him in slow motion, he moved to the side so that when the blow landed, it hit the trunk of the tree which was behind the prince a second ago. The prince lifted his sword and brought it down on his friend's neck. Before the sharp blade could come into contact with Yala's neck, there was a blur of movement and someone had pulled Yala out of the way. The blade swished through the air and fell harmlessly on the ground.

The prince cried out in astonishment and fury. A slender figure dressed in black turned around to face him defiantly and the prince finally recognized the pale face—it was Jade. Raja Perita snapped, 'So you were the one who lured me to the temple that night!'

Her lips twisted into a little smile of conceit before she said, 'Yes, it was me; it was not difficult to fool you, my lord!'

He replied coldly, 'We shall see about that!' He picked up the sword and strode purposefully towards the two of them. By now, the wounded Yala was too tired to fight back. Jade realized that this was no longer the hot-headed young man who rushed into danger, this prince was cold and calculating and would no doubt kill both of them. She cried out, this time in fear, 'Please don't kill him! I love him! We were only doing the bidding of the Dark Lady!'

The prince nodded towards Satra who immediately threw him the spear he was carrying. The prince caught it expertly in his hand and threw it in a single movement—it flew through the air with a whistling sound, pierced through Yala and pinned him to the tree. He screamed in agony while Chula and Satra looked on in shock. The prince spoke to Jade, 'If you want to live, I suggest that you leave this place now!'

She fled into the forest, still weeping in anguish. The prince walked towards his friend and pulled out the spear. Yala fell to ground, lifeless. Now that his anger was spent, Raja Perita felt overwhelmed with sorrow. He wondered how one of his best friends in the world could grow to hate him so much. Finally he roused himself to address his two friends, 'He did not turn into a monster by himself. There is another one that I must deal with tonight,' he said. There were tears of blood flowing down his cheeks.

Chula and Satra nodded without saying a word. They knew he was referring to the vampire in the ruined temple. Chula finally spoke, 'You must not weep any more, my lord. Enough royal blood has been shed . . .

Yala brought this on himself when he drew his sword. And he lied to us all; I've learnt enough from my father to understand that it was all about gaining power; he intended to usurp the throne while the King lies in a trance. Now we must bury his body with the proper rites before it gets too dark.'

They buried their friend as best as they could and set out on their journey. Raja Perita said, 'I don't need Yala to show me where to find her. She made me into what I am and I am always tied to her in a subtle way.'

When they approached the champaka grove, he turned to his friends and said, 'I command you to stay outside the circle of trees, no matter what happens to me. The demon has supernatural powers and no mere human can stand up to her.'

He crossed decisively into the grove and walked towards the ruins. Even before he came close, he heard a silvery laughter. He recognized it immediately and felt a chill of fear run down his spine. Raja Perita looked up and saw the very same woman who had changed his life so horribly. She had not changed at all since he last saw her. Enraged, he sprang at her and seized her by the neck. She gasped and prised open his hands and threw him across the clearing. He went hurtling for some distance but managed to recover his balance.

Chula and Satra, who were watching from a distance, held their breath. They had only glimpsed the dark maiden briefly in the prince's first encounter with her, and had sometimes wondered if they had imagined it. But seeing her shimmering with dark energy, filled them with utter horror. Chula whispered, 'The prince will not survive this encounter and neither will we.'

Satra replied, forcing himself to speak, 'The prince will prevail. Everything he has gone through has made him stronger . . . he has to.'

They jumped when she shrieked at the prince, 'How dare you attack a priestess of Nirrti! The handmaiden of the goddess who haunted cemeteries, the dark forests and the caves in hills.'

He said coldly, 'You chose to become this vile demon! I did not! You took my life away and changed me into a vampire! I should cut off your head right now.'

She laughed coldly and said, 'I chose this life? I had nothing to do with it. A poor maiden who was taken from her home and family in order to become a handmaiden to a goddess associated with misfortune, pain and death. The maiden had no choice, really. Because of the position of the stars at the time of her birth, it was her fate to keep misfortune away from the kingdom by serving the dark goddess.'

Her voice dropped and was tinged with sorrow, 'But she did the best that she could to serve her goddess and the kingdom, eating parched rice and drinking sour milk to keep herself alive; but one night she was taken by brigands and offered as a blood sacrifice . . . but the dark goddess brought her back and she avenged herself by killing all of them.'

She shuddered and continued, 'Their blood was everywhere, but by then she had turned into a vampire. She needed blood to survive.'

Raja Perita felt his heart sink when he heard her story. She was a victim after all, just like him. Who was he to judge her?

The handmaiden continued, 'She was very beautiful; it was not difficult for her to persuade a rich and adventurous nobleman to marry her and to take her along with him to the land across the sea, even though it was taboo. A few of the sailors in the ship died during the journey but no one suspected the woman. She found herself in a land rich with rice fields and fruits, but people began to be suspicious when the people around her started dying, including her husband. Of all the people I've killed, it was his death I regret the most.'

Her voice grew cold in anger again, 'Yes, they drove me to this temple and cast a spell to imprison me here.'

He hardened his heart and told himself that it was either her or him, there could never be two predators in Langkasuka. He lifted his sword and strode towards her with cold determination. She managed to evade his attack but his sharp blade managed to cut off a lock of her hair. She shrieked in rage, 'Do you really think you can kill me, princeling? I, who was created even before your puny kingdom came into existence; and given life by a goddess.'

Then she sprang at him, teeth bared and claws extended. Although he leapt aside, her sharp claws racked one side of his face and the pain made him drop his sword. But the prince managed to grab her arm and flung her towards the trees.

She struggled to get up and speak, 'Wait . . . in return for your blood, I gave you the gift of immortality! The ability to slow time itself. What more could you want, young prince?'

He replied grimly, 'I want my life back, vampire! I want to be able to walk in the sun. I want things to be what they were before I met you!' He picked up his sword and walked grimly towards her.

She said to him, with what seemed almost a tinge of regret in her voice, 'I'm afraid it's too late now, Raja Perita died on that fateful night when we first met and was reborn as Raja Bersiong. Why would you want to return to that dreary old self?'

As she spoke, she walked with fluid grace towards the edge of the clearing. Her movements were so mesmerising that before Raja Perita realized what she was up to, she had drawn near to Chula and Satra who were standing just outside the grove. She turned towards them and smiled. She said softly, 'Come closer, young lords! Let me take a look at you!'

Taken by surprise, Chula and Satra could not stop themselves from looking at her in the eyes. The truth is they were watching the handmaiden in a mixture of dread, fear and fascination; she was after all unlike anyone or anything they had ever come across. In an instant, they fell completely under her spell. Raja Perita called out, 'No! Don't go near her! Stay where you are.'

But the two young men had been mesmerized and compelled to do her bidding. They stepped across the magic circle and were within her grasp. She gripped them both by their wrists.

Raja Perita felt as if his legs had given way beneath him and he fell to his knees. He realized that he had no choice but to give in. Even if he could destroy her, she was right—he could not return to his old life. He dropped his sword and said in a defeated voice, 'Please don't harm my friends, they are everything I've got. I have no family, no kingdom, nowhere to go any more. Everyone fears and despises me.'

She replied, 'At least you have your friends, princeling. I, on the other hand have been alone for a very long time. You brought this upon yourself, you allowed people to learn of your secret. Our kind must always remain hidden. We live in the shadows and we only come out at night to feed and we never allow people to know our true selves.'

He rose on his feet and walked towards her unarmed. When he came close to her, he said, 'I am unarmed; you have nothing to fear.'

She released Chula and Satra and drifted towards the prince, her eyes glowing in the dark. She knew that when he was unarmed, she could easily overpower him. Raja Perita reached out, held her by the arms and pulled her closer to him. She smiled and her lips curled back to reveal her fangs. She took his cold pale face in her hands and said softly, 'I've been waiting for someone like you for a long time. I cannot escape this magic circle without your help. You, however, can break the spell. Then when you have learnt how to use your true powers, my lord, we will have the entire world at our feet.'

Then she noticed that his eyes were glowing like live ember and realized that something was terribly wrong. Her life force was ebbing and she felt cold, as cold as she had been the night she was dying. She cried out in terror, 'Noo . . . What is happening to me? Release me.'

She clawed at his hand and struggled to escape but his grip was strengthening even as she was weakening. She screamed, 'I am your maker! Release me, or we both die.'

He said grimly, 'You were wrong about me, Padma. I am not dead. In fact I've never been more alive!'

She managed to gasp, 'How did you know my name.' But her skin was slowly turning ashen and her raven-black hair was turning silvery grey as she felt her life force draining away. Raja Perita finally released her and the temple maiden collapsed to the ground.

The spell on them broken, Satra and Chula ran towards the prince. Chula was the first to speak, 'The fates be blessed that you are all right! Is she dead?'

Before he could reply, Satra asked, 'How did you do it? How did you manage to kill her?'

Raja Perita said quietly, 'She is not dead . . . just in eternal sleep.' He paused and added, 'Come, help me to put her back in the temple.'

Both Chula and Satra registered surprise at his request but they knew better than to question him. They helped him to lift the handmaiden of Nirrti and carry her back into the ruined temple. Hidden inside was a series of steps which led to an underground chamber. They found what looked like a hollow stone crypt and placed her inside. Then they climbed up the stairs and walked outside. The three of them moved some large stones, remnants of the old temple, to block the opening. He said, 'As long as no one awakens her, she can do no harm.'

Chula finally asked him, 'Why didn't you kill her?' Satra nodded in agreement and echoed what Chula said, 'Yes, my lord, Perita, why didn't you kill her?'

He replied sombrely, 'She was as much a victim as I was. When I held her and took her life force, I also took some of her memories. She was doomed to serve her dark goddess because of the alignment of the stars during her birth. Although she was decked in fine jewels and clothes, she led a miserable life as the handmaiden of Nirrti, who was apparently a goddess who accepted parched rice and burnt coconuts as offerings. But her fate took a turn for the worst when a group of cruel men abducted her from her temple and offered her as a blood sacrifice. They unwittingly unleashed a curse because the dark goddess turned her into a vampire and she killed all the men who attempted to harm her and in successive nights turned on the villagers who were kin to these men.'

Satra was clearly moved by the story while Chula looked sombre. He felt compelled to point out, 'We agree that she is a victim, and suffered terrible injustice at the hands of evil men. But she is a dangerous creature. What if someone in Langkasuka manages to wake her up? My lord, there may be no one to stop her murderous rampage the next time.'

Chula looked at the prince in the eye to make sure that he would not attempt to evade the question. Even Satra turned to look at the prince; after all the dark priestess had almost killed all of them.

Raja Perita replied calmly, 'Chula, no mere human can wake her up; it will take a being with tremendous life force to do that.' The prince added, 'I feel empty . . . utterly devastated. I've killed both my childhood friend and my maker in one night . . . and I'm not sure if I can live with these memories . . .' his voice trailed off.

Chula saw the anguish in his eyes and felt something akin to despair overcome him. For once, he could not find the words to comfort the prince. He had gone through too much himself and he was still trying to understand what had happened in that long night.

It was Satra who spoke, 'My lord, Perita, if you can't live for yourself, then live for us . . . and your mother and father . . . because we need you more than ever.'

Raja Perita got up and walked to the scene of the battle, collected his sword and told them wearily, 'We will hide for a while on Mount Jerai where the hill tribes, who are my mother's people, will protect us.' Chula and Satra lowered their head in silence as they followed him into the forest surrounding the temple.

The Village on the Hill

The prince accessed the memory his mother had shared with him and found the almost invisible path which he knew led to the village on top of the hill. They made their way through almost pitch-black darkness under the canopy of the trees and the prince was thankful for his preternatural senses. The journey became much easier when he located the stream, from the gentle bubbling sound it made and they followed it upstream. The stream was lined with bamboo, and he heard whispers urging him to hurry up. When they were nearing the village, Raja Perita said, 'I sense that the sun is about to rise and we have to hurry,' and redoubled his pace.

Chula and Satra, who were some distance down the path were too exhausted to keep up. Chula called out, 'Please go ahead, my lord . . . we will catch up soon.'

The prince did not have far to go; Tok Batin was waiting for him near the summit of the hill. She was accompanied by a few men. She recognized Raja Perita at once and broke into a smile. She ran to him and greeted him with an embrace, 'Welcome home, my beloved grandson! How happy I am to see you; you are so like your mother! Welcome indeed! But now we must hurry to the village because the sun has risen in the valley.'

She seemed to know exactly what was going on and did not wait for any explanation. The men hurried him into the nearest hut in the village, as the first rays of the sun reached the summit of the hill.

When Chula and Satra finally arrived at the village, they found Raja Perita asleep in a hut, being tended to by a tall and stately elderly woman. They had already guessed who she was when she introduced herself and welcomed them to the village. The two of them gratefully accepted the sweet drink they were offered, made from the sap of the palm tree. Then they wearily lay down beside the prince and promptly fell asleep as well.

The three young men rested, here in this faraway village, where the air seemed fresher and purer, the sun brighter during the day and the night sky clearer than it could ever be in Kota Aur. Chula and Satra took part in the simple everyday life of the villagers, mainly days spent in gathering food from the surrounding forest and the occasional hunt for small game. They shared the simple food of the villagers and slowly healed in body and soul. The prince, who slept during the day, would lay under the clear night sky and bathed in the moonlight. On clear moonless nights, he watched the river of stars circling him in the sky. When he bathed in the stream, he heard whispers from the surrounding bamboo grove and glimpses of shimmering figures moving among the bamboo. He did not attempt to approach them and they left him alone. Every evening, Tok Batin prepared for him a special broth made from the roots of various plants, with bamboo shoots and the leaves of the red *bayam*. In the first few days after he arrived, she added animal blood to the broth but reduced it over time. He was also allowed to drink a concoction made from the sap of the palm tree which the villagers kept aside especially for him. The sweet drink kept him from feeling hungry at night and the prince slowly lost his dependence on blood.

Sometimes his friends joined him to gaze at the moon and the stars. They had lost track of time and only knew that time was passing from the waxing and the waning of the moon. They wondered why they had never noticed how incredibly beautiful the night sky was.

On one such night, Raja Perita said out loud, 'Do you miss, Kota Aur?'

Chula replied, 'Oddly, enough, I do. I mean, I love it here . . . the village has helped me to heal . . . and I believe to become whole again. But I miss the palace and the culture . . . and the comforts of civilization.'

Satra said, 'Me too. Compared to this place, Kota Aur is chaotic and stinking, but I'm beginning to miss my family and the people and . . . the food; especially spicy food, so much . . .' He added quickly, 'I mean, I'm grateful to Tok Batin and the villagers for allowing us to stay here. I'm beginning to feel like myself again . . . my old self . . . after so long. What about you, my lord?'

The prince was silent for a long while. Finally he replied, 'I'm delighted to hear that you are both ready to return to Kota Aur. Tok Batin has informed me that my father, the king, has awoken from his trance . . . apparently some months ago.'

Chula interjected, 'That is wonderful, my lord!'

The prince continued, 'Tomorrow, some men from the palace will be here. You are to go with them—Chula to take your place as Maharaja Lela and Satra, to head the army and to train the new warriors of Langkasuka and also to explain to my mother and father, why I am unable to return.'

Chula and Satra sat up abruptly and turned towards him. Chula said, 'My lord, Perita, you cannot mean this. You have to return to Kota Aur and the palace. You are the heir of Langkasuka!'

Satra protested, 'My lord, we will not return to Kota Aur without you. I have sworn to protect you with my life.'

'Chula, according to Tok Batin, my father is fully recovered, so Langkasuka does not need an heir anytime soon, and I release you from your vow, Satra. My mind is made up . . . I cannot return to the palace!' Raja Perita's voice was resolute.

'So you chose to abandon us, my lord,' Satra said quietly. Chula was silent. Seeing their hurt expression, he explained quietly, 'Please understand that I can't return . . . the palace will remind me of Yala . . . I will see his shadow and hear his mocking voice, everywhere I turn . . . and I will see the ghosts of Bujang, Rawan and Maharaja Lela . . .' his voice trailed off.

They bent their head in silence. Finally, Chula said, 'Very well, my lord. As always, your wish is my command, but I truly hope you will return to Kota Aur one day and . . .' He had to stop speaking because his voice was breaking.

Satra was too distraught to say anything.

The men from the palace arrived in the village, in the afternoon of the next day. They rested for the midday meal and then started the journey downhill, with Chula and Satra. They were told that Raja Perita had left the village a few days ago and would not be returning to Langkasuka.

* * *

Raja Perita remained at the village until it was once again the night of the full moon. He put on his warrior outfit, which had been carefully washed, dried and kept aside by Tok Batin since he first arrived. The prince walked to the stream, accompanied by Tok Batin. A small *sampan*, similar to the one his mother had used a long time ago, was waiting for him. He said farewell to Tok Batin, who blessed him with the words, 'May you always carry the peace of the hills in your heart, my grandson, and remain strong and humble!'

Raja Perita said, 'I will always remember you and your kindness, Tok Batin,' and kissed her hand.

She reminded him again, 'Your need for blood may grow again, once you are far away from the hill. But the yakshi in the bamboo grove strengthened your ability to draw sustenance from the living things around you. Use that ability without harming living things, take only what you need to live.'

He nodded and climbed into the *sampan*. There was a wooden plank across the middle of the *sampan*, which served as an uncomfortable seat but Raja Perita preferred to stand. Tok Batin was slightly startled but he seemed so sure, she said nothing. A streak of silver moved through the bamboo grove fringing the stream and slipped into the water. The *sampan* moved swiftly and steadily downstream, with the prince balanced perfectly on it. He felt exhilarated as the cold wind blew at his face and through his hair. He threw back his head and laughed out loud, feeling truly alive.

The rushing stream became larger as it was joined by other streams until it was a river. When it reached the estuary where the fresh water of the river emptied into the salt water, the silver streak which had been guiding the *sampan* pulled away, whispering to him, 'I can go no further, you have to guide the vessel now. Stay safe, Perita, and return to us when you are able to.'

Raja Perita bent down to pick up the oar and debated on whether to row the *sampan* or to just swim into the open sea. However, a head bobbed up from the water and a young boy emerged beside the *sampan*. He said with a wide grin, 'My lord! Give me a silver coin and I will take you to wherever you want!'

'Me too! You will need my help as well, my lord! My brother can't do it alone.' Another head bobbed up; this time it was a young girl from the sound of her voice.

Raja Perita guessed they must be children of the Orang Laut, the sea gypsies, more at home in the sea than on land and had the ability to remain underwater for extraordinary lengths of time. He pointed out to sea, 'You see that five-masted *perahu*? Take me there!' and he tossed a silver coin to the boy and another to the girl. They each caught a coin deftly in their hand but did not bother to climb into the *sampan*; instead they pushed it while swimming!

The boy said, 'The Orang Laut do not row *sampan*, we swim faster than any *sampan*.'

The *sampan* reached the side of the *perahu* with surprising speed and came to a standstill beside it. The children waved at him and swam away towards the shore.

Without hesitation, Raja Perita grasped the rope ladder hanging on the side of the vessel, pulled himself up effortlessly and quickly clambered up on to the deck. It was late night, so most of the sailors manning the vessel were asleep along both sides of the deck. A gentle breeze blew, smelling of seaweed and the sea; he could taste the salt on his lips. There was no fear that the sleeping men would awaken, the waves lapping against the vessel, which rocked gently in rhythm with the sea, would ensure that. He walked silently on the deck, drawing energy from the sleeping crew and putting them into an even deeper slumber. But he remembered Tok Batin's advice and made sure that he did not take too much. They would wake up a little more tired than usual. He headed unerringly towards the cabin—the most opulent one. A faint light came from the curtained window along the side. He opened the door and slipped inside.

Despite the slightness of the almost imperceptible sound, Princess Chaiya, who was asleep on a silk covered divan, opened her eyes. The slight rush of sea breeze into the cabin when he had opened the door, had awakened her. She sensed a presence in the room and stealthily reached for the dagger, kept in a recess in the cabin wall beside her bed.

She barely dared to breathe. She was more than capable of fighting a man, why did she feel such overwhelming terror? Gathering all her courage she jumped out of her bed on to the wooden floor, her movements as swift and graceful as a cat. She stood on her bare feet, dressed in a loose muslin tunic, her slender figure silhouetted in the moonlight. The moon beams from the window also caught the glint of silver of the embroidery on the sleeves and hem, and the dagger in her hand. She could not see him but she knew that he could see her. She tried to say something but she had lost her voice; she couldn't even scream.

Raja Perita stepped out of the shadow and said in a slightly ironic voice, 'Have you forgotten me so quickly, my lady, Chaiya? We were supposed to have been married months ago.'

There was a shocked stunned silence. She recognized his voice instantly, barely daring to believe what she was hearing. Perhaps she was dreaming. Was the tall dark silhouette really him? She stood rooted to the spot, her heart pounding, her muscles tensed and ready to strike. But as her eyes adjusted to the darkness, she was able to make out his pale features and strange bright eyes in the moonlight. A huge wave of relief washed over her when she realized that it was really him, her beloved Raja Perita. She allowed herself to relax, but only a little, still unsure if she could trust him. She finally found her voice and whispered, 'My lord . . . is it really you? They said that you were gone . . . that you would never return to Langkasuka . . .'

'Not to Langkasuka but I would like to visit Palembang . . . you did invite me to view the astounding

Torona of Sri Vijaya, that magical evening in the Moon Garden. Or have you forgotten, my love?'

Raja Perita took a step tentative towards her. He sensed her fear and he dared not touch her, knowing that it would be she who would be the one who would decide.

She took a deep breath. He was now close enough for her to notice that he looked thin, almost gaunt, but the haunted look was gone from his eyes. She said, 'And is that all you're interested in, my dear Lord Perita? Visiting the vidhyadhara-torana at Palembang?'

He laughed softly, 'No jewel-encrusted bridge could entice me to visit a country, my dear Lady Chaiya! Not without you in it! In fact, I don't mind living as a forest dweller, as long as you are with me.'

She smiled at his reply. But something else occurred to her. 'What about your friends, my lord? Could you bear to part with them? You loved them so much,' she asked anxiously.

Unexpected tears formed in his eyes. 'Yes, I did love them; but I had to kill one of them, and I couldn't live being reminded of that . . .' his voice broke.

The dagger dropped from her hand to the floor with a slight clatter. Tears sprang to her eyes and she wiped them with her night dress. 'I'm so sorry, that you had to go through so much, my lord . . . I thought I would never see you again . . . I missed you so much.'

She reached out with her hand and he took her hand in his. Their fingers intertwined.

'And I missed you . . . my love, Chaiya. I thought it might be safer for you if I stayed away, but I've learnt something about myself in the last few months—I can live with humans and other living beings without harming them,' he replied softly. 'Do you think you could bear to live with a monster like me?' his voice was uncertain.

'You're not a monster to me . . . you never were. I've loved you from the moment I met you, my love,' she replied, reaching out to touch his cold cheek with her other hand. He took her hand in his and kissed it.

She drew closer to him, looking him in the eyes as they embraced. They held each other tightly for a long time, drawing comfort from each other's touch and when they kissed, his umber eyes glowed slightly in the dark but so did hers. Yaksha embraced yakshi.

Acknowledgment

First of all, I would like to thank Nora Nazerene Abu Bakar, Associate Publisher at Penguin Random House SEA for accepting my manuscript for publication and thus allowing me to be associated with the most iconic brand in the world of publishing.

I would also like to thank Rajni George, the Development Editor, for her insightful comments and suggestions, which helped me to take the story further and give fuller expression to this tale of *The Blood Prince of Langkasuka*.

I would also like to thank Neelima P Aryan for the brilliant cover design for the book.

It would be remiss of me not to thank Gerakbudaya, the publisher who arranged to have the manuscript Beta-read. Even though they neglected to follow-up, the review made me realise I was not barking up the wrong tree and made me persevere with my writing and making further submissions.

I also thank everyone who has nudged the book towards this direction and who was involved in the production of the book.

And finally, I would like to thank the readers who deign to pick up a book by minority, POC and diverse writers.